MW00917289

THE SPINDLE OF FATE

THE SPINDLE OF FATE

AIMEE LIM

FEIWEL AND FRIENDS
NEW YORK

A Feiwel and Friends Book
An imprint of Macmillan Publishing Group, LLC
120 Broadway, New York, NY 10271 • mackids.com

Library of Congress Cataloging-in-Publication Data is available.

First edition, 2024
Book design by Maria W. Jenson
Feiwel and Friends logo designed by Filomena Tuosto
Printed in the United States of America by Lakeside Book Company, Harrisonburg, Virginia

ISBN 978-1-250-88619-4
1 3 5 7 9 10 8 6 4 2

For Stanley, my brother and best friend,
who believed the most

What do you think happens when we die, Keanu Reeves?

I know that the ones who love us will miss us.

—Keanu Reeves on *The Late Show with Stephen Colbert*

ONE

Everyone Needs to Stop Calling the House!

Adults are so weird about death.

Just look at some of the "helpful" things people have said to me and my sister since Mom was declared dead:

1. "She's in a better place now." What am I supposed to say to that? "Yeah, it sucks that they still haven't found her body, but the ocean is cool. She always wanted her ashes to be scattered there someday anyway!"
2. "At least it was peaceful. Drowning is like falling asleep." This isn't true. I looked it up and wish I hadn't because it turns out drowning is, in fact, *a really scary way to die*. But now I can't unread that, so thanks for that, Uncle Mark.

3. "This is why it's so important to be healthy so you can live to a hundred." To be fair, this was said by my Auntie Lilli, who will look at any food you put in front of her and immediately tell you whether it prevents or causes cancer. (Nothing is cancer-neutral, apparently.) But Mom woke up at 6:00 A.M. every day to run in the park and used low-sodium soy sauce and it didn't do her any good, so if anything, this just shows you that it doesn't really matter.
4. "The important thing is that she loved you." This one is a little better because it's actually true. I know that just like I knew every time I opened my lunch box, there'd be a handwritten note reading *You can do well if you work hard! Love, Mom.* Always the exact same words ever since my first day at kindergarten. But the thing is, it was just as true ten days ago, and back then, Mom was still alive. So I don't see how that's supposed to make me feel any better.

We finally had the funeral three days ago, but the weird old landline phone in the living room is still getting calls from family members and family friends, including some I've never heard of before. I know they mean well, calling to check in on us. And I guess I'd be mad if they *didn't* call. But it's starting to get on my nerves because we're *also* getting calls for our tailor shop downstairs. It doesn't reopen until next week, but since we already have a two-week backlog—not to mention all the orders that we already had and were left unfinished when we closed—Dad's started taking them so he wouldn't be totally bombarded on Monday. He also started putting the phone on speaker so he could cook at the same time. All morning has been an endless series of sympathy calls mixed with: "Hem these pants." "My jacket is missing buttons." "Make me this dress from the internet." "When are you reopening? Sorry for your loss."

Over the weekend, my grandma had been coming over to help Dad out with the house, but today Āh Mā had to go back to work at the beauty salon. So I woke up to find two to-do lists stuck to the door of the room I share with my sister. I just picked up our last load of laundry from the laundromat next door, so I only have a couple items left on mine. My best friend, Thida, said she'd stop by after lunch, and I won't know exactly when that is because I don't have my own phone yet and I told her not to call the house. But it's almost one, so it should be soon. I just need to power through a little bit longer.

"Oh, come *on*, Mona Li." I groan when I come back into the living room, only to find the laundry basket containing the previous load still unfolded. My eight-year-old sister's list of chores was just a Post-it note, but all she's gotten done are four socks. Not four pairs. Not even two pairs. Four single, unmatched *socks* folded in half. Very neatly, to be fair.

"It's not my fault! My hands are small," Mona Li whines. The uncut bangs of her bowl cut hang in front of her eyes, so she has to keep swiping them aside. Dad usually takes us to get our hair cut a couple weeks before school starts, but Āh Mā said we're not supposed to cut our hair until after the mourning period is over.

"What does that even mean?" I reply. My voice comes out angrier than I meant it to, and it freaks me out. After we drove home from the funeral, Āh Mā made us stop at a random McDonald's and all get out to use the bathroom, so the bad death vibes wouldn't follow us home. Now that I think about it, it seems kind of messed up to just dump said vibes in a public restroom, but I just wanted to go home already, so I didn't question it. Āh Mā and Auntie Lilli then took me aside by the ketchup dispenser and told me that as the oldest, I have to "woman up" and be strong for my dad and my sister now. But even if growing up means no more skateboarding with Thida on Saturday mornings because I need to do chores, I'm still too young to be *snapping about chores.*

I take a deep breath and try to calm down. A few weeks ago, I could just roll my eyes and tell my sister not to be so sensitive, but things are different now. I don't want to be like the callers, trying to help but just being another problem for Dad to deal with.

And then the phone rings again, and I imagine snatching it right out of my dad's hands and hurling it out the window. But our apartment is on the second story above the tailor shop, which is right across the street from the second-most popular boba shop in downtown Avalon. I don't want to accidentally hit and kill a pedestrian. Their family might hunt me down for revenge, or spam us with one-star reviews on Google.

"Reliable Quality Tailoring," says Dad in the kitchen. "Oh, sorry, Auntie Susan—"

Even though Dad's family hasn't lived in America as long as Mom's side, his Chinese is a lot worse than hers. He speaks Mandarin at about a first-grade level, or maybe a second grader who is not very bright for his age, if you're feeling generous. So he takes his calls in mostly English with the occasional broken Chinese, which means a good number of both the customers and the family friends hang up pretty quickly. But it also makes it harder for me to block out the ones that don't. I grind my teeth as I listen to him explain to Auntie Susan that it's very nice of her to call but he's making lunch right now.

"Wow! You cook?" Auntie Susan says over the speaker phone. She's not actually my dad's aunt, but a friend of my grandma's that he calls "auntie" out of respect, just like Mona Li and I do to all Chinese adults.

"No, not really," Dad admits. "I mean, I could make instant noodles okay in college, but . . . well, it's been a while. I've been learning with YouTube, though."

Dad took care of most of the housework while Mom ran the business. The exception was cooking. Āh Mā never taught Dad how to cook, because according to her, he was "too handsome" to need to learn to make his own food. That seems super weird and sexist to me (not to mention really insulting to my Uncle Kenny, who she did teach to cook). But Mom thought it was the funniest thing ever. She would ask Dad to help her with something in the kitchen and then go, "Oh, sorry, I forgot you can't cook because you're *too handsome*."

Literally two seconds after Dad hangs up, the phone rings again. "Reliable Quality Tailoring," Dad says. His voice is so dead, you'd think he just got back from his own funeral. "Oh, hi, Mark."

I squeeze the necklace around my neck tightly. It's basically just a red string but tied into an elaborate pendant of interconnected knots and loops, like the red knot decorations that we hang up for Lunar New Year. Mom made it for me before I was born, and she and Mona Li and Auntie Kathie have ones, too.

I have my own chores to take care of. I don't have time to do all of Mona Li's, too. But maybe she just needs a nudge to get started. Grudgingly, I fold a pair of pants in half, then toss it on the floor for her to fold again.

Pouting, Mona Li looks down at the butterfly-print pants in front of her. "Mom made that for me," she sulks.

"Well, yeah. Mom makes—made all of your clothes."

I realize and correct my mistake as soon as I say it,

and immediately wish I hadn't. Mona Li's lower lip starts to quiver.

Oh no.

"EVIE MEI!" Dad shouts suddenly from the kitchen. "Can you come over here?"

My insides twist. Dad doesn't get mad, ever. The first time I ever heard him yell at someone was last week, when Uncle Kenny told us, "Everything happens for a reason."

Sucking in my breath, I fling my braid over my shoulder and head to the kitchen. Dad is washing his hand in the sink. I follow a lot of YouTube channels about how to make movies, and there was one about how CGI humans are always so creepy because they're *almost* lifelike but not. That's how I've felt looking at Dad ever since Mom died.

"Hey, Robin," he says, and some of the tension leaves my body. Dad calls me that because when I was little, I liked to play with him like we were Batman and Robin. But then he adds, "Just got to smile through the pain."

He's been saying that a lot lately. I think it's supposed to make me worry less about him, but now every time he smiles, I can tell he's dying inside.

"Could you go down to the shop and get some

dollar bills from the register? I'm going to order food and I need to tip the driver."

"I thought you were cooking lunch?" I almost make a joke about how he's too handsome for this, but I stop myself. Normally I would joke around with Dad, but I don't know if it'd make him feel better or if reminding him of Mom's old joke would only make him upset. That's been happening a lot lately: I don't know what to say that won't be useless or worse, so I just end up not saying anything. Mom was always telling me that I could get straight As if I just thought through my answers a bit more, but now I have to think about *everything* and I hate it.

"Uh, yeah . . ." Dad looks down at his hand, still under the running water. Suddenly I notice the huge cut on his finger. He manages a smile, and I feel like throwing up.

I stuff the still-incomplete chore list into the pocket of my shorts and turn toward the stairs. At first I'm relieved to get out of here. But when I put my hand on the rail, it hits me that I haven't been down to the tailor shop since Mom died.

I tell myself I'm being dramatic. There are lots of things I haven't done since Mom died, and I can't just freeze up before every single one of them. I'd never be able to do anything. I roll my eyes at myself to emphasize how silly I'm being, then grip the railing and walk down the stairs to the shop.

I switch on the lights. Everything is as organized as a museum exhibit, like usual. When I look over toward the cash register, there's still a bowl of guava candies on the counter and a potted bamboo plant by the door, which I hope is still alive considering no one's watered it since Mom was reported missing. To my shock, my nostrils even catch a faint whiff of my mom's favorite banana milk body lotion. It's a smell that used to relax me, but it's like even my muscles know it's not the same. The usual *rat-a-tat-tat* of the sewing machine is gone. The only noise in the room comes from the *tick-tock* of the clock and my own breathing.

Suddenly my unease about coming down here disappears, replaced by a weird kind of relief. It might be musty and full of painful memories, but at least it's quiet. Mom had the shop soundproofed a couple years ago so her work wouldn't wake us up. I could set off firecrackers and Dad wouldn't have any idea.

I shut the door behind me, then take a deep breath and scream.

It feels even better than I thought it would, to be able to just explode and not have to worry about anybody asking me if I'm okay. I fill my lungs up with air one more time, then scream loud enough to drown out a hundred well-meaning relatives, "AND NO ONE CARES THAT IT'S MY BIRTHDAY!"

Oh, yeah, I didn't mention that besides being three days after my mom's funeral, today is also my twelfth birthday. I haven't said anything to my family because I don't want to be sulking about my birthday when there are obviously more important things going on. But after getting call after call from anyone who even vaguely counts as a relative and not a single "happy birthday," it's hard not to feel a little petty.

When I open my eyes again, I see that the bamboo is actually fine. Āh Mā said bamboo is pretty much unkillable, and I guess it's nice that something is. But hanging above it on the wall is Mom's calendar, which is still turned to July. Ten days since Mom thought she'd be right back, since her car was found in the ocean. I still don't understand how that even happened. She was as careful and precise behind the wheel as she was with a needle and thread. Dad used to say that she always drove like the cops were right behind her. But somehow she ended up in the water—or at least, her car did. Search and rescue never found her body, so we had to get dressed up and make a big fuss about an empty box. For a while Dad tried to keep the shop running, but as the days piled up and they never found her, they eventually stopped searching.

As fast as it appeared, any relief I had is gone, here and gone just like that. Like Mom. My muscles tense back up as my own thoughts surround me. No, the silence isn't relaxing down here. I just feel alone.

Maybe down here I can scream and whine and cry all I want and no one will care. But then I have to go back upstairs to give the money to Dad, and I can't do those things upstairs. I need to "woman up." But at the moment, all I can bring myself to do is lean back against the wall, breathing in and out, clutching Mom's pendant like it might just disappear on me if I let it go.

Then I hear a *bang*!

TWO
Are You Afraid Of . . .

My eyes burst open. At first I think I must have accidentally knocked over the little home altar with my dead grandparents' photos that sits in a nook in the corner of the shop. But when I look over, it's still there. A shiver runs down my spine.

I flash back to when I was little, when I was convinced for a while that the tailor shop was haunted. Back before we had the place soundproofed, I would sometimes hear my mom's sewing machine in the middle of the night and thought it was a ghost. When I told Mom, she told me not to worry about it because "ghosts only bother people who believe in them."

Why am I thinking about ghosts? It was probably just a small earthquake. Unwinding my shoulders, I look around the shop, just to make sure nothing's broken before we officially reopen for business tomorrow.

I glance at the back wall, where spools of thread are mounted. They're organized by color—unlike my mom's closet, which is sorted by material—so it's easy to tell just by looking that nothing fell off. On the opposite end is the clothing rack with suits and jackets and dresses hanging in plastic bags. Doesn't look like the noise came from there, either.

Along the side wall are three parallel worktables. Mom didn't have any employees, unless you count Dad, so they're just extra workspace. I spent a lot of time here doing my homework at the back table before I was old enough to watch myself upstairs. But I never just sat here watching Mom sew the way Mona Li did. It annoys both of us when customers assume that as the oldest, I'm going to "take over the family business" someday.

Dad can alter and mend just fine—he's not *great* at anything like Mom was, but his secret superpower is that he can learn to do just about anything really quickly. He'll probably be a pretty good cook by the time school starts. But his work is more Reliable than Quality. Will people still come to us for things like fixing up wedding dresses without Mom?

As I check behind each of the sewing machines and cones of thread in the work area, I remember

Dad is waiting upstairs. I head to the counter to get the money and, sure enough, I find Mom's thread book overturned on the ground. Mystery solved.

I bend down and pick up the "book." It has an indigo cloth cover embroidered with an image of the Cowherd and the Weaver Girl, this Chinese love story that Mom told me and Mona Li all the time when we were little. But when you open the book up, the "pages" are swatches of fabric folded into dozens of intricate boxes that can be tugged open, like a pop-up book. Mom uses the boxes to store her threads and needles and buttons.

I gather up fallen spools and pins from the floor and tuck them back into the compartments neatly and carefully, the way Mom would have done it. It always made me impatient whenever we'd play family board games and she'd take forever to get the pieces lined up perfectly. I almost got banned from game night when she was on my team and I complained that if she spent less time straightening the board and more time thinking about her next move, maybe we'd win for once.

It's kind of funny. Mom's perfectionism really annoyed me sometimes, and now she's gone and I'm straightening all her things for her.

The last thing I put back in the book is a family photograph. Mom loved physical mementos, maybe because she worked with her hands. This picture was from several Halloweens ago: Mom always made us the coolest Halloween costumes, and for a couple years now Reliable Quality Tailoring has been offering custom costume services in October. That year was Studio Ghibli costumes. Mona Li was Kiki from *Kiki's Delivery Service*, and I was San from *Princess Mononoke*, with a fake fur cape and mask and everything.

Without meaning to, my eyes go straight to Mom's tiny face, smirking as she poses with her creations. She wasn't really smirking, but she didn't like showing her teeth because one of her front teeth was crooked, so in photos she always looked like she was. Her chin-length hair is permed and meticulous, without a strand out of place.

Suddenly, my eyes start to sting, like when it's fire season and there's smoke in the air. My hand shakes as I slip the photo inside the front cover. Exhaling, I press all the page compartments flat so the book closes shut, then get up to put it back on the counter. But when I do, I find myself staring at a hunched figure, sitting on the countertop and peering at me.

Its face is so white it's almost bluish, with beady black eyes and a flat, almost skull-like nose. The rest of its body is covered with striped golden fur.

It's a monkey. In our shop. Less than six inches away from my face.

I almost cry out with alarm, but I clamp my hand over my mouth. I don't want to startle it and set it off. (I know I said this birthday is total trash, but you know what it really needs? *Rabies.*) Swallowing, I back away slowly. But before I can move toward the door, the monkey bares its fangs at me and screeches louder than a fire alarm.

I hurl myself backward before it can lunge at me and nearly fall into my mom's swivel chair. My heart racing, I climb into the chair and, with a forceful kick, push myself back all the way across the room. But then the monkey jumps toward me, and I realize I've literally backed myself into a corner.

I scramble behind the dress form torso Mom uses—used—to fit clothing, next to the threefold full-length mirror and supply shelf. I pull free the pair of scissors on the shelf. Feeling like a little kid putting chopsticks between my fingers and pretending to be Wolverine when we would go out for dim sum, I grip the scissors between my knuckles with one hand while holding the mannequin torso out in front of me like a shield with the other.

"I don't want to hurt you," I say. Because if I tell the monkey I don't want to hurt it, then it'll understand and just leave me alone, obviously. Gulping, I glance at the door on the other end of the room. I could try to make a run for the stairs, but I don't want the monkey to follow me into the apartment and bite Dad or Mona Li. On the other hand, I can't just sit around trapped in a room with an angry primate, either. I have to take a chance.

When the monkey skulks closer, I push the dress form at it. It screeches as the mannequin torso falls over on top of it and knocks it to the ground, but the form is just made of foam, so it shouldn't really hurt it. Bolting to my feet, I turn to make a dash for the door while the monkey is down.

But then I hear an "Ow! That hurt!"

I stop in my tracks and turn around very, very, *very* slowly.

The monkey climbs up from under the dress form, rubbing its head where the dummy torso bonked it and muttering, "I was just trying to wish you a happy birthday."

My first reaction is that I must be dreaming. For

a moment I feel a surge of excitement: If this is a dream, maybe *all* of this was a dream, and when I wake up, Mom will still be alive.

I take a deep breath, then slap myself across the face as hard as I can. But when I open my eyes, my face hurts and the monkey is still blinking at me. Still talking, too.

"That was . . . odd," it remarks, peering at me like *I'm* the freak of nature.

As it dawns on me that I'm not dreaming, my stupid hope melts away instantly, like a vampire in the sun. But then it hits me again that I'm *not dreaming*. Which means that a monkey *just wished me happy birthday*.

"How did you . . ." My voice seems to have gotten stuck inside my throat. "How did you know it's my birthday?"

As soon as I hear my own words, it occurs to me that is *maybe* not the strangest thing about this situation.

The monkey purses its lips, as if it's amused by the question. "Well, you did just scream about it quite loudly a minute ago. Scared me to death." Its face looks too human when it talks, which makes the fact that *it's talking* even more unsettling.

"*I* scared *you*?" I say. "Five seconds ago I thought

you were going to eat my face! Why couldn't you have just said 'happy birthday'?" My voice comes out higher and squeakier than usual, which would normally be embarrassing, but I'm too busy worrying that I might *literally* have gone mad with grief.

The monkey squats onto the fallen dress form. It hits me that I blew my chance to make a run for the door.

"It was funnier," it replies matter-of-factly. I glare at it, but it just lets out an annoying, screechy laugh. "You can call me Uncle Monk."

Yeah, no way I'm calling him "uncle." I'm used to calling random adults Uncle or Auntie, but I draw the line at monkeys. This can't be real. "Um, okay," I say. "And, uh, what are you doing in our shop?"

"I'm looking for your ma. And while I'm here, I thought I'd drop off your birthday present."

"You liar!" I blurt out. "My mom is . . ." Heat rushes into my face, and I swallow. But seriously? *I know your mom?* That's some textbook stranger danger right there.

"You just said you knew about my birthday because I yelled it just now," I said, trying to sound smarter than I feel. "How would you have a present for me?"

"I was just kidding," Monk says. I might have been

skeptical before, but I can't argue with that totally convincing and not at all suspicious explanation. "Of course I'd know your birthday. My present for you is right over there. See?"

He gestures with his tail. I roll my eyes, because that was literally what Liam McDermott did before he cut off my braid. And even in second grade, I was embarrassed to fall for such an obvious bully trick. Sighing, I shift my eyes in the direction that the monkey is pointing at, careful not to turn my head.

"Made you look!" Monk cackles like a six-year-old who just said the word *butt*. "But no, seriously, I really do have a present for you. It's over—"

But I've already seen—and heard—enough. The second he turns his head to point, I charge forward and grab the scruff of his hairy golden neck. He screeches as I throw open the closet door, just behind us on the wall, and shove the squealing monkey inside.

THREE

A Message from the Dead

I slam the door shut before Monk can open it, then grab the spare key from the top shelf on the wall. *Got you!* I think triumphantly as I lock him inside.

"Hey! Let me out!" Monk bangs on the door. Exhaling, I reach up to put the key back on the shelf and notice a large square box. Across the room, I'd thought it was cardboard, but up close I realize it's actually wrapped with crinkled brown paper—obviously reused—and tied with red string in a bow. Mom would *never* do such a shoddy job wrapping a present.

Frowning, I inspect the box. Tucked underneath the string is a hóngbāo, a red envelope with the character for "good fortune" embossed in gold on the front, just like the ones I get from my relatives and sorta-relatives on birthdays and Lunar New Year. On the package are the words *Happy birthday Evee Mei, from Uncle Monk* written in red ink. His handwriting is surprisingly decent, even if he did misspell my name.

Huh. So Monk *did* know it was my birthday. Could that mean he was telling the truth about looking for Mom, too? But why?

I flash back to what Mom told me about ghosts. By that logic, does that mean she believed in talking monkeys? She wasn't as dismissive of ghosts and superstitions as Dad, but she always seemed weirdly... practical about the supernatural. Mom would go to temple every Lunar New Year to pray for good fortune for our family and the shop, but she always declined to have her sticks thrown by the fortune teller. She said that if she could change her fate, then she'd do it herself, and if she couldn't, then there was no point worrying about it anyway.

I glance back at the closet, Monk still screeching inside and banging on the door. When I open the red envelope and find a crisp two-dollar bill, I feel a little bad about locking him up. Sure, he was being really annoying, but he did wish me a happy birthday. But even if he wasn't lying about this, he was still suspiciously vague about everything else. If I can't trust him to give me a single straight answer, I can't trust him to just wander around in our apartment.

Guess I don't have to go to the register after all. I tuck the red envelope back under the string, then dash back upstairs with the package under my arm.

When I burst into the living room, I find Dad has left the kitchen and is pacing around the living room, checking his cell phone. "Here you go," I say, panting and handing him the two-dollar bill. "Uh, Dad, I have to show you something . . ."

"Evie! What were you doing down there?" Dad says. "The delivery driver's almost outside!"

He looks up from his phone, and even though it wasn't my fault that a talking monkey was running amok downstairs, I can't help but feel bad anyway. Dad looks exhausted, and his forehead is covered with so much sweat, I could wash my hands with it. Obviously I wouldn't, because that's gross, but I could, which is also gross.

He looks . . . bad. And his mom isn't the only person who says my dad is handsome. I've been told that he looks like four different members of BTS, which is more than half of BTS. (This feels low-key racist, because I don't think he looks like literally any of them, but whatever.) Auntie Kathie always laughs about how people kept telling Mom how lucky she was to marry him, until she got sick of it and snapped,

"No, he's lucky to marry me." Mom could be a little bit full of herself.

But I mean, she wasn't wrong.

Suddenly, I don't have the heart to tell him about the talking monkey who claims he knew Mom. Not now, when he's already dealing with everything else. It might break his brain. As he runs to the door, I quietly take my single birthday present to my room.

"Evie?"

Mona Li opens the door. Like Mom, my sister doesn't wait for me to respond before entering.

"Thida's here," she announces, and it feels like an elephant just got up off my chest.

Thida Hnin might not seem like she would be the most supportive best friend. She won't laugh at people's jokes if she doesn't think they're funny. One time we were binge-watching all the *Dead Reckoning* movies and I asked her if she would be able to chainsaw me if I got bitten by a zombie, and Thida said, and I quote, "Yeah."

But she's come to our apartment every single day since Mom was reported missing with Burmese food her parents made for us. She just stays here, even though I haven't really wanted to talk or do anything.

And she does it without saying meaningless words that she doesn't even know are true, like "Drowning is peaceful" or "Everything happens for a reason." With my best friend here, I can figure out how to deal with Monk without having to bother Dad.

I toss the box onto my unmade bed and pull the comforter over it. Mom was always trying to get me to make my bed because she read somewhere that people who make their beds are more likely to be successful. When I told her that doesn't mean making the bed will make you successful, just that people who make their beds are probably try-hards, her response was, with logic like that, I was sure to be successful if I only tried harder, for example, by making the bed.

Mona Li looks down at her small feet. "I was going to make you a hat for your present. Mom was going to teach me to use the hand loom."

Oh. Of the two of us, my sister was always the one more interested in Mom's craft. I couldn't even thread a needle when I was Mona Li's age, but she was so eager to learn that Mom taught her early. She's really good at it, too. When the COVID-19 pandemic started she sewed face masks for our entire extended family, and she was *four*. My sister really should be the one to take over the tailor shop someday, not me. If the business will even last that long without Mom.

Once again, I have no idea what to say. I don't want to say something stupid like "That's okay," because nothing about this is okay. I don't really see how anything can be okay ever again. But I can't say that, either, or at least not to my little sister.

"Not that you care," Mona Li mutters.

Where did *that* come from?

"Hey, what's that supposed to mean? Just because I don't cry as much as you doesn't mean I'm not sad, too."

Mona Li's lower lip trembles, and she clenches her fists. For a moment I think she's going to punch me, but then my sister looks me straight in the eye and says, "You keep complaining about the fake things people have been saying since Mom d-died, but you're just as bad! You complained about Mom to Thida all the time before. So don't act like you're sad now."

She storms out into the hallway. The door slams shut, and I just stand there, shaking.

It's true that Mom and I hadn't always gotten along lately. Even before we started arguing, I'd never been a "When I grow up, I want to be MY MOM" kind of kid, like my sister. But that doesn't mean I didn't love her just as much as Dad and Mona Li. I might not know why Mom died, or if she really is in a "better place" now, but I know how much I loved her.

But did Mom know?

"Evie?" Hearing my best friend out in the hallway, I open the door. Then I stuff my hands into my pockets before Thida can see that they're still shaking.

Thida comes in. Dad says she reminds him of John Lennon from the Beatles because of her shaggy hair and round glasses. Her Hawaiian shirt in highlighter colors lifts my mood just a little. Dad, Mona Li, and I can't wear any bright colors until a week after the funeral. We're also not supposed to wear anything red for forty-five days, since red represents happiness and good fortune. But I refused to take Mom's pendant off. Dad just told me not to let Āh Mā see, so I've been wearing it under my shirt.

"Happy birthday!" Thida unzips her clear plastic mini-backpack and takes out a wrapped box with *Happy 12th birthday, Eevee* written on it in Sharpie. She spells my name that way because that's my favorite Pokémon. For my seventh birthday, exactly five years ago, my parents took me to Build-A-Bear just to buy the Eevee plush and then Mom made an outfit for it herself.

"Thanks, Thida. But listen, I need to tell you something." I blurt out the entire story about the monkey and the mysterious package sitting on my bed. When I'm finished, Thida has that look that she gets when she's about to tell me something I don't like.

"I know what this sounds like—"

"Like the time you were convinced Mr. Fernandez had murdered his wife and you tried to dig up the kickball field?"

Okay, sometimes, Thida's bluntness can get on my nerves. Like when I told her about my two-step plan to become a movie director by making one really acclaimed indie movie and then getting hired by the MCU, and she told me it was "not that easy." If I wanted to talk to someone who's not going to believe in me, I would have told my parents.

"But this is different. I saw it with my own eyes—"

"That's literally what you told me about Mr. Fernandez."

Thida will never let me live that down. But here's the other thing about her: Yeah, she told me so. But she also helped me dig up the kickball field anyway.

"Okay, fine," I say. "But I don't think I'm imagining it this time. I'll show you."

I close the door, then yank off my comforter, unveiling my mysterious present. Thida sizes it up. "So . . . after you locked the monkey in the closet, you found this just sitting on the shelf?"

She still sounds skeptical. Intrigued, but skeptical. That annoys me a little, but I guess a random box doesn't necessarily prove anything.

"Yeah." I reach out to pick up Monk's gift, but then realize I'm still holding Thida's. It'd be kind of messed up to put down her present only to open a different one from someone else, even when that someone is a talking monkey, so I open hers first. It's also wrapped in reused paper, but in, like, a cool, sustainable way.

"Oh, this is awesome."

"I know, right? It only cost four dollars, too!" Thida got me a really cool vintage halter top from the 2000s. Her big sister likes to take me thrifting because I've picked up enough tailoring knowledge to sniff out the quality finds from the fast fashion stuff that Mom called "landfill fodder." Mom really didn't like me buying secondhand, though. She was already upset when I said I wanted to start picking out my own clothes instead of wearing the old-fashioned things she made for me. She had really good taste, but I just didn't want to dress like my mom.

I flash back to Mona Li calling me out. Sucking in my breath, I turn my attention back to my only other present. I tear off the wrapping to reveal a cardboard box, and Thida and I peer inside to see . . .

Another, smaller, wrapped box.

I stare at it for half a second before understanding hits me like a dodgeball. "He did *not*," I say as I tear off the wrapping paper to find . . .

Yes, he did. Inside that box is another, even smaller box. Groaning, I unwrap that one and take out an even smaller box. As I repeat the process with box number four, I'm wondering what's the smallest one that I can stuff Monk into, when I open my present *again* to find . . .

At the bottom of the box is another red envelope.

"That's weird," I mutter. "He already gave me one."

I open it, and for a moment, I'm afraid I'm going to see another, smaller red envelope inside. Instead I find a little cloth scroll, tied together with red string. I unfurl it to find words embroidered in tiny, even red stitches.

Help me

Ive been taken to Diyu, the netherworld where people pay off their debts for the bad things they did in life. But I am not dead.

Im sorry. I thought I could escape but had no spool. Find me in Diyu.

PS Happy birthday Evie. I know you can do well if you work hard!

I read through most of the message with my eyebrows furrowed. It's only when I make it to the end that I suddenly understand, and my whole world unravels.

FOUR

See No Evil, Etc.

Thida blurts out, "Is this some kind of sick joke?"

I pull my eyes away from the even stitches to gape at her. "What? No, it's not. You think I would *joke* about my mom being alive?"

But would the monkey? To my horror, I realize that does seem like something he might do. But . . . would he really? There's "making you look" and there's telling a kid whose mom just died that actually, she's still out there. Monk was annoying, but could he really be that cruel to do that to someone he doesn't even know? What reason would he even have to lie about something like that?

"That's not what I mean!" Thida taps on the scroll. "I know your mom's a seamstress, but why would she *sew* you this message, instead of just writing one?"

"Maybe—maybe she didn't have a pen." That's weak and I know it, and Thida looks at me in disbelief.

"You can't seriously believe this, can you?"

Thida's words make me flinch, but I can't blame her. I mean, I just spent the last week fact-checking whether my mom's death was painless. Can I believe that my mom didn't really die? That she was taken to . . . the netherworld? I know I shouldn't, but I mean . . . there's already a talking monkey in my basement. Is this really any weirder than that?

I read the scroll again, not just because of what it says, but because I shouldn't be able to read it if this is all a dream (which is still the only logical explanation I can think of for all of this). I know that from watching old Batman cartoons with my dad—there's an episode where Batman is trapped in a dream, but he figures it out because whenever he tries to read books or the newspaper, the letters are all jumbled. I think it's because you dream with one side of your brain but you read with the other side or something.

But no, I can read the scroll. I still don't completely understand what it means—I have no idea what the part about "no spool" has to do with her not being able to escape. But I can read the words, which means this is *not* a dream. Which means either the talking monkey locked in the downstairs closet faked this note for some weird reason, or . . . this really is from my mom.

But as I finish reading the hand-sewn message again, I realize Monk couldn't have faked this. Because Mom made sure I would *know* this is from her.

"This is really her," I say finally. "My mom put notes in my lunch at school, and she always signed them the same way: 'You can do well if you work hard.'"

When I was little, I never got sick of reading the same message from Mom in my lunch every day, just like I never got sick of her telling me the story of the Cowherd and the Weaver Girl every night. Later I'd started resenting them, seeing them as a constant reminder that I could *do better* at school or at tailoring if I only *tried harder*. But now I find myself choking up as I read the familiar words aloud.

Thida chews her lip. When she can't think of a reply to that, she says, "Okay. But if your mom's alive, then what's she doing in the . . . netherworld?" Thida frowns. "It sounds like that's . . . uh . . . the 'bad place'?"

Mom never really talked about what she believed—*believes*, I realize, heart pounding—happens after people die. When religious people try to give her pamphlets, she pretends she doesn't understand English, even though she was born in California just like Dad. So I don't really know what the netherworld even is. Could this all be some kind of huge mistake somehow, like some *other* Dawn Liu Huang was supposed to die and my mom was taken instead?

The irony would be almost funny if it weren't so horrifying. Turns out she's not in a "better place" after all.

But then I realize that's actually *better*. Because it means Mom is alive, and I just have to figure out how to get her out.

"I don't know," I say. "But there's someone downstairs who does."

Thida and I sneak downstairs and back into the tailor shop.

"Wait," Thida says, before I can step toward the door. "What kind of monkey did you say he was? If he's actually a chimp, he could definitely take both of us. They're stronger than us and really vicious. They have wars just like humans."

My mom didn't really like Thida, because she's smart but lazy, which according to Mom is somehow worse than being stupid and lazy. I've never told Thida about this, and I'm never going to, but it's one of the reasons we'd been fighting more.

I almost thank Thida for that unnecessarily upsetting animal fact, but I appreciate that she's thinking about how to deal with Monk like he's real and not just a figment of my imagination. "I don't think he was a chimpanzee. I threw him into the closet pretty easily."

"Still, should we have weapons or something? Even if the monkey didn't want to hurt you before, it might be mad now that you've locked it up."

I imagine opening the closet door only for a shrieking, furious Monk to spring out at me. Wincing, I nod. "Good idea." I circle the work area and pick up Mom's plastic pink three-ring binder with all her records. Thida, meanwhile, has already grabbed the iron from the board in front of the clothing racks. She likes to roll her eyes and act like the voice of reason, but I think there's a part of her that secretly likes doing things that make no logical sense, even if—maybe even because—she knows it's a bad idea. I think that's part of the reason why she always goes along with all my ideas eventually.

Taking a deep breath, I unlock the closet door and swing it open slowly. When Monk doesn't jump out at us, I relax, but then freeze.

There's no one in the closet.

Thida turns from the empty room to me. Her grip relaxes around her iron, but the rest of her body is tense as she says slowly, "Evie . . ."

"He was *here*," I say stubbornly, trying to convince myself as much as Thida. I can't have imagined this. I know I can't have. I know I thought I did before, but if the monkey was never here, that would mean Mom's note . . .

Suddenly, Monk appears out of nowhere and snarls at me, long fangs bared. I almost fall over in shock, but Thida grabs my shoulder at the exact same time, pulling me away from the mad monkey . . .

. . . which then falls backward into a ball, laughing.

"Got you," he says, blowing a raspberry. There's a loud *thunk* as Thida drops the iron. But Monk doesn't seem to notice or doesn't care. "Oh, don't look at me like that. You're the one who locked me in an airless closet and then ditched me."

He glares at me with his beady black eyes. "If this is how you treat someone wishing you a happy birthday, I'd hate to see how you treat your enemies."

I put my hand over my chest, trying to calm my racing heart. "I was going to come back," I huff. "Look, thank you for the hóngbāo, but you were really freaking me out, okay? You know, what with being a talking monkey in my basement and all."

"That's another thing! I'm not a *monkey*." Monk scoffs. "I'm a demon that just *looks* like a monkey."

"Oh, now it all makes sense," Thida says. Despite her attempt to play it cool, she keeps blinking, like if *this* time when she opens her eyes, the talking monkey—or not a monkey—will be gone. I'm too horrified to take this rare chance to be the one saying "I told you so" for once, though.

"You—you're a *demon*?" I say, spluttering.

Monk sighs. "Yāoguài—'demon' might not be an exact translation. Basically any kind of supernatural being. We're not all bad. Okay, most of us are, but that's true of humans, too."

That seems kind of harsh, but I have more important things to do right now than defend my species. "I opened your gift," I say, changing the subject. I take out the scroll from my pocket. "How did you get this? Why is my mom in . . . Dìyù?"

Monk makes a face, like my trash Chinese pronunciation causes him physical pain. "As I was going to say before you locked me up like an unwanted dog, I'm a supernatural private investigator. I was hired to find your ma and the Spindle of Fate."

I stare at him blankly. "Spindle of Fate?"

For a moment, Monk actually shuts his mouth. He blinks at me, like I just said I didn't know what water is.

"Your ma didn't tell you about the Spindle?" When I shake my head, he looks dumbfounded. "Did she tell you about the Guilds? The Weavers?"

I shake my head.

"You're not joking with me, are you?" Monk says incredulously. He strokes the golden hairs on his chin like a wizard or an old master in a martial arts movie might stroke his beard. "All right. Your mom was the head of a secret society known as the Weavers. For centuries, your mother's family and their students devoted themselves to mastering the secret art of weaving magic."

"Okay, hold on," I blurt out. "You're telling me my mom was the leader of . . . of some kind of weaving cult?" How would she even find the time? Even in the early days of the pandemic, when our business almost completely dried up (and that started months *before* the stay-at-home orders), Mom somehow seemed to find *more work to do*. It was like she couldn't keep her hands still or she'd go bonkers. My dad liked to say she's like a shark: If she stopped moving, she'd—well, you know. More than once during quarantine, I'd hear her footsteps going down the stairs in the middle of the night, as if she was going to the shop to work on nonexistent orders . . .

Huh. I'd chalked up Mom's inexplicable night shifts to her being what Auntie Kathie called "a workaholic going into withdrawal." But what if she'd been doing work for her mysterious side gig?

"You could show a little more respect, you know." Monk sniffs. "Under your family's tutelage, the Weavers could produce all sorts of magic string: threads of good fortune, love, magic, and even time. But your ma wasn't merely their leader. She was also the master of the Spindle of Fate, which can change a person's destiny."

This conversation reminds me of Monk's trick boxes, each question opening up another and another. I'm impatient to get to the only question that really matters—how do I get my mom out of Dìyù—but also . . . my mom had the power to *change fate*? Kind of makes me wonder why she even bothered to tell me to work hard, then.

"Now, as you might guess, there are a lot of people out there who would do anything to change their destiny. And one of those people sent a yāoguài—an evil one—after her. The demon ambushed her, then dragged her to the Courts of Dìyù and threatened to leave her there unless she did what it asked for."

My hand seeks out Mom's pendant. I take a deep breath and force myself to focus on one question at a time. "Just to be clear, that's basically, like . . . the *bad* place where people go after they die, right? Like fire and eternal torture and stuff?"

"Well, there's plenty of torture, yes. But it's not eternal. You serve your time, and then you get reincarnated into the next life and hope you do better next time."

"Oh, so it's like Buddhist Hell," Thida pipes up.

Monk nods. I stare blankly at her, and she explains, "In Buddhism you have multiple lives, so 'Hell' is technically more like in-between lives rather than an *after*life. You don't spend time there forever, just to pay off any bad karma. Chinese Hell must work the same way."

I guess that's a nice idea, that you can get a second chance instead of being screwed forever. That does nothing to make me feel better right now, though. "My mom went missing ten days ago," I say, my throat suddenly dry. "If she's still down there . . . does that mean she didn't give in?"

"I don't think that woman knows how to give in. After the yāoguài dragged her down there, she did something it didn't expect: She ran away." Good for her, I think, until Monk says, "She ran *into Dìyù*, taking the Spindle of Fate with her! And since the netherworld is a massive underground torture labyrinth ten layers deep, the yāoguài has about as much chance of finding her as a maggot in a hill of rice."

And there I was thinking that Buddhist Hell sounded kind of chill. Like, people just meditate and think about what they've done until they're free to go or something. Nope: My mom is lost in a *massive underground torture labyrinth*.

Swallowing, I ask, "If she's lost in Dìyù, how did she send me this message?"

"That's old Weaver magic: sending writing across distances through needlework. They'd carry these special handkerchiefs around and sew messages into them, and then hundreds of lǐ away, another Weaver could whip out their own handkerchief and read it. Kind of like texting before phones. Of course, that's precisely why the Weavers stopped needle-writing, but naturally your ma still knows all the traditional crafts."

That does sound like Mom, who loves *super* vintage stuff. Monk holds up the scroll. "I found this in a pile of random junk gathering dust in the shop—she must have hoped there was a chance someone would see it."

Alarm bells go off in my head at Monk's casual admission that he was sneaking around before, too. But I'm more disturbed by the idea that Mom's distress call might have been sitting down here all this time, and we didn't notice it.

But then I frown. Pile of random junk? Gathering dust? In *my mom's shop*? That might be a weird thing to question after all the stuff about Mom having power over fate through some kind of string-based magic, and I guess I obviously didn't know her as well as I thought I did. But the Mom I knew did not do *mess*.

Something about Monk's story isn't adding up.

"Who did you say hired you again?" I ask.

"That's classified information." When I narrow my eyes, he continues, "Like I said, I was hired to find your mom. But I might have left something out. I was hired to find her *before* she disappeared, not after. And I *did* find her."

I frown, feeling like I'm trying to figure out a riddle. But then Monk's skull-like face stretches into a demonic grin as he reveals the answer: "I'm the yāoguài that took her to Dìyù."

FIVE

A Deal with the Yāoguài

Monk bursts out laughing. For a moment, I think—I *hope*—he's made a seriously messed-up joke.

But then he grins, and not in a *ha-ha-made-you-look* way. Like a demonic way. And I realize he isn't joking.

"You . . . *you're* the demon that took my mom?" I say, spluttering.

"I said yāoguài aren't all bad. Which is true, by the way. But I never said I was one of the not-bad ones."

He belly-laughs again, and I want to strangle him with his own tail.

Thida says, "And you're just telling us this now . . . why?"

"Same reason I spent all that time wrapping those

boxes. It was funny." No one else laughs. "But also because your ma gave me the slip in Dìyù. So now I need the string she gave you to find her."

Monk's tail shoots forward and slaps the scroll. "I didn't find this message in the shop. I found it in her car before I pushed it off the cliff. The spool she's talking about is another Weaver trick—you take a spool of thread and let it fall, and it'll lead you straight to where you need to go. But you need special Weaver thread, and since I don't have time to look at every piece of string in an enchanted tailor shop fronting as a regular tailor shop, that's where you come in."

"Me?" I say. "But I didn't even know about any of this until five minutes ago."

"When you were born, your ma made you a red string necklace, right? That's no ordinary string—it's a protective talisman and *very* magic."

My blood runs cold, but it's already too late—my hand had leapt to my neck the moment he mentioned my pendant. "Don't worry, I'm not going to rip it off you. That'd break the enchantment," Monk says nonchalantly. "Which is why I need you to hand it over."

"And why would I do that?" I say with disgust.

"Because unless we can find your ma, she's stuck in Dìyù. And if she dies down there, it'll be for real."

I had been ready to flip over the tables in the workroom, to scream at Monk that he'll never take me alive like I'm in an action movie. But suddenly I get a sinking feeling in my stomach as I realize that Monk's right.

Monk holds out a fluffy golden paw. "If you help me, okay, the bad guy's evil plan worked, boo-hoo. But you'll get your ma back. If you ask me, that's really not a bad trade."

I can't help the demon who kidnapped my mom . . . can I? What if that's the only way to get her back?

BONK!

My conflicted thoughts are loudly interrupted by the sound of Thida smacking Monk across the face with the iron. The yāoguài slumps to the floor, knocked out cold.

"Thida! Why did you do that?"

My best friend stares at me incredulously. "Seriously? You can't help him! What if whoever hired him to kidnap your mom wants to become president and nuke Canada or something?"

I look at the yāoguài at my feet. If Monk wanted me to do anything else, I would be literally kicking him while he's down for what he did to my mom. But now all I can think about is how whenever Mom can't make a decision, she'll flip a coin. Not to make up her mind for her, but because the moment she lifted her hand away and saw which side the coin had landed on, she would know what she had really been hoping for. That's how I feel looking at Monk's unconscious body: Even though it's stupid and maybe even selfish, I know now that I *really* wanted to say yes. Yes, I'll help you, even though you took my mom, if it means I can get her back. I'll do anything.

I know Thida is right. But I can't leave my mom there. I can't lose her again, knowing that I could have done something about it.

I look at Mom's message again. *Find me in Diyu.*

Even in my desperation, I know that just marching into Dìyù with a piece of string is a bad idea. The spool might be able to show me where she is, but there's still the whole *massive torture labyrinth*. Who knows what kind of horrifying dangers are down there? But Mom clearly wrote this message hoping it would be seen by someone who'd understand what "had no spool" meant.

I really don't believe that Dad could have known about any of this. He always said he doesn't believe in the supernatural, and maybe this is childish, but I don't want to believe that he might have been lying to me, too. That leaves my mom's side of the family, which is just her little sister, my Auntie Kathie.

"Monk said my mom's *family* were Weavers, too." So why didn't I know about it, then? But I set my feelings about that aside for now. "Maybe my Auntie Kathie was one, too. She's working from home right now, so we can go to her apartment and show her Mom's message."

Thida tilts her head. "Isn't that your aunt who's a showgirl in Las Vegas?"

"She's a showgirl on cruise ships now, but she moved here to be closer to us after she got pregnant. And she's a seamstress, too. Like, she used to fix up her costumes by hand. She and my mom both learned from my grandpa, so she probably knew about all of this, too."

I wait for Thida to sigh and tell me all the reasons why I'm not thinking straight. But for once, she doesn't even pretend to try and discourage me. She just says without hesitating, "Go get your skateboard. I'll take care of the monkey demon."

Heart pounding, I race upstairs. But before I can

return to my room, Dad intercepts me in the living room.

"Hey, Robin," he says. He waves his hand to get my attention, revealing his finger is now bandaged. "I'm sorry it took so long, but I finished making lunch."

Making lunch? "I thought you ordered takeout?" Isn't that why I went down to the basement and found the yāoguài in the first place?

When I glance toward the dining table, I spot a familiar lavender box next to a bowl of fried rice and a Tupperware container with Burmese curry from Thida. Even before Dad says "Surprise!" in an upbeat voice, I know what's in the box: my birthday cake. I always get the same cake every year, mango mousse from the Taiwanese bakery down the street.

Suddenly, I feel like a baby for being so angry that everyone "forgot," even just in private. Still, if I'm going to save Mom, I have to get going.

"Uh, actually, Dad, I was going to go skateboarding with Thida. I can eat cake when I get home, maybe after dinner?"

"Oh . . . okay," says Dad. "I'm sorry I was so late with lunch."

He looks guilty, which makes *me* feel guilty for

making him feel bad. But I remind myself that if I can get Mom out of Dìyù—and I have to—I'll be able to blow out the candles on my birthday cake with my entire family.

"It's okay," I say. I help myself to some fried rice, partly to make Dad feel better and partly because it's almost one thirty and I really am hungry. Auntie Kathie's house would be about a half hour away on our skateboards, so as impatient as I am to head out, it probably is a good idea to eat a quick lunch at least.

"Well, you don't have to go out in black in this heat," Dad says as I devour my fried rice. It's not as good as Mom's—Dad put too much egg and not enough chicken—but it's not bad. "It's not like I'm gonna tell Āh Mā on you."

According to Āh Mā, I don't *have* to wear black, but most of my stuff has a bright color or print, and since I just did the laundry I didn't have a lot of options. Dad looks at my black T-shirt and PE shorts and winces, which is the same reaction I have every time I look at his mourning outfit. He's also wearing a black T-shirt, only his has an awful, personalized caption: HARDER, BETTER, FASTER, HUANGER. It's the worst thing Mom ever made, maybe even the worst thing *ever* made, and I know from her eye roll when she gave it to him for his birthday last year that it pained her a little bit to stitch those words. But she knows how much Dad loves Daft Punk and horrible puns.

Suddenly I feel sorry for my sister, who's going to have a serious style downgrade this fall if Dad has to take her back-to-school shopping instead of Mom making new clothes for her. Mom is always mocking the quality of retail clothing in general, but she especially hates how ugly and ill-fitting the clothes are for kids with larger bodies like Mona Li. It'll be like she had a movie makeover montage but in reverse. But then I remind myself that Dad won't have to take care of that. Not if I bring her back.

I finish eating most of my rice, then pour myself another glass of water from the pitcher on the counter. "Hey, Dad?" I say as I power walk my empty plate to the kitchen sink. I should get going, but I can't help myself. "Do . . . do you believe in fate? Or destiny, or whatever?"

I'm 99 percent sure he doesn't and that trying to convince him that Mom was taken to the netherworld because of her magic ability to change fate would be a waste of precious time at best, and at worst, get me rushed to the hospital for some kind of evaluation. On the other hand, if you'd asked me earlier, I would have definitely said I was 100 percent sure that Mom had not been taken to the netherworld because of her magic ability to change fate, so.

But then Dad's forced smile disappears, and I know at least one of my parents wasn't lying to me. "No. I don't."

He says it just like that, without even thinking about it, like when Thida told me she'd totally chainsaw zombie me.

"What Uncle Kenny said . . . Look, your uncle meant well, but . . ." He shakes his head, and I remember his very un-Dad-like response to Uncle Kenny telling me and Mona Li that "everything happens for a reason." As scary as it was to see him yelling like that, though, I kind of agreed with my dad. If everything happens for a reason, would that mean that Mom *should* have died? Like it must be a *good thing* somehow? Even if fate is a real thing—and I guess it is, if Mom could change it—that doesn't mean I have to accept that.

Dad takes a deep breath. Forces a smile again. "There's this story that my dad, your Āh Gōng, told me when I was a kid about an old man whose horse ran away."

I always liked asking Dad questions when I was

little because he has this way of answering with stories. I used to bombard him with every random question I could think of, like what superpower would he want to have, or whether he would save me or Mona Li first if the apartment was on fire. Even though I should probably excuse myself and get my skateboard, I can't help but listen.

"All his neighbors went, 'Hey, sorry, man, that's unlucky'. But then the horse came back with another, wild horse. So then his neighbors said, 'Wow, that was lucky,' but then his son rode the new horse and it threw him off and he broke his leg. So his neighbors said, 'Wow, that was unlucky.' But then China was invaded, and the emperor put out a decree that all able-bodied young men would have to join the army. And since the son was injured, he didn't have to go and his life was saved."

I furrow my brow as I consider his story. "So the moral is, if something *seems* bad . . . maybe actually it's good, because something good will happen later?" Then what's the point of doing literally *anything* if you have no idea if it'll be a good or bad thing?

"Yeah, I didn't really get that story, either. But now I think I understand it more. It's not like the horse ran away so someday his son would live. It's just that life is unpredictable, and to get through, we kind of have to accept that we don't really know how anything turns out until it's over."

Dad scratches his temple. "So this idea that things are 'meant' to happen the way they do, that it's all for the best in the end . . . yeah, I don't know. It always seemed kind of self-centered to me, to be honest. It's just another way for fortunate people to tell themselves that they must have *deserved* their good fortune somehow."

What my dad is saying makes more sense to me than "everything happens for a reason, so we should be happy with that even if they're really bad things and we can't see what those reasons could possibly be." But at the same time, it seems super depressing to think that bad things—like my mom suddenly dying, or being kidnapped by an annoying monkey-like demon—could just happen for *no* reason.

Dad must sense my lack of satisfaction with this answer, because he smiles. With his eyes. "When I was in high school, I was going to go to this party, but I ended up staying home because I got sick. My friend who was supposed to drive me got into an accident and didn't wake up for a month. I was convinced that it must have meant something that I hadn't gone, that my stomach bug was some kind of divine intervention. But then Auntie Lilli gave me a reality check. 'If the universe was going to do someone a favor, why would it be you?'"

"Wow. Auntie Lilli roasted you."

Dad laughs. "I mean, she was right. Now whenever I get a little too ahead of myself, thinking things are going to work out for me just because, I remember that. 'If the universe was going to do someone a favor, why would it be me?'"

He pauses. "There was only one moment in my life that felt meant to be," he says softly.

"When?"

"When I met your mom."

For a moment, the mask slips. But then Dad's cell phone rings, and he shakes his head.

"I should have known. 'If the universe was going to save someone, why would it be me?'"

He plasters on a smile as he answers the call. "Reliable Quality Tailoring."

I contemplate Dad's story as I return to my room and retrieve my skateboard, along with my helmet and wrist guards. Maybe the universe has no reason to save my dad, but Mom would. If Mom really does have the power to change fate, could she have been the one to prevent Dad from getting into that accident, before they even met? Or was it just a coincidence?

I'll have to ask her when I see her.

One last thing. I shut the door and change out of my sweaty black shirt. Then I throw on a red lifeguard tank top I found thrift shopping with Thida.

I'm not supposed to wear red after my mom's death. But my mom isn't dead, so it's okay.

SIX
FAMILY BUSINESS

When I come back to the living room, I spot Mona Li, still hunched over the laundry. I consider walking around her to get to the fire escape, then decide that I'm not going to be scared of my baby sister. Even if I am still rattled by our conversation earlier.

"I'm heading out with Thida." It comes out like an apology, even though I know I didn't do anything wrong. But why does it feel like I did?

Mona Li just carries on not folding the laundry as if she didn't hear me. That stings more than I want to admit, but I have more important things to do than prove to my sister that I'm hurting, too.

I'm in such a hurry to get out of here, I practically throw myself down the fire escape. I think it's safe to say that no one who ever lived has been as eager to go to Hell as me.

When I arrive outside, I find Thida, her acid-green skateboard slung over her shoulder. Her other arm is wrapped around the biggest box from Monk's package.

"Is that . . ."

"The demon? Yeah." As I get on my skateboard, Thida walks over to the trash bins that had been left out on the curb for pickup. "The garbage truck should be on its way soon, so that's convenient."

She props open the lid of the black bin and shoves the box containing the yāoguài inside. This is why we're best friends.

"That's cold. I love it."

We skate out of downtown Avalon and toward the residential area, where my aunt lives. "So your mom's been magic this whole time and she didn't tell you?"

Classic Thida, ripping the Band-Aid right off so hard, it opens the wound right back up.

"No, she really didn't." But as my thumb rubs against my red string pendant, I suddenly flash back to Mom teaching me to knot good luck charms out of a single thread for Lunar New Year. I always got restless and bored when she tried to teach me handicrafts, partly because I'm not that interested and partly because Mom's perfectionism makes it not fun to learn. When she realized I wasn't doing a good job because I was clearly not trying that hard, she became impatient, telling me the good luck wouldn't work unless each knot was done perfectly.

I'd rolled my eyes, thinking that was just an old superstition that my mom didn't even believe but was just saying to be annoying. But was it possible she'd tried to teach me Weaver magic, and I'd just zoned out because I didn't take it seriously and wasn't paying attention?

Twenty minutes later, we pull up into the apartment complex where my Auntie Kathie is staying while she's in Avalon. She used to be a showgirl in Vegas, and then after her show shut down she got a job dancing in shows on cruise ships, so she spent the entire previous year traveling the world and living on different cruises. But she hasn't been able to renew her contract since she became pregnant, so she moved back to California to be closer to us. Mom wanted her to stay with us, and I got really excited for a couple of days, but Auntie Kathie's response was, and this is a direct quote, "I love you, jiějiě, but if I have to live with you, I will not love you anymore." Which sounds harsh, but I have a sister, too, so I get it.

I step off my skateboard and walk up to Auntie Kathie's first-floor apartment. The porch is covered with pairs of shoes of different sizes.

"Is your aunt having visitors?" Thida asks, glancing at all the shoes.

"I guess?" I have no idea who they would even be, though, since my aunt hasn't been staying here all that long. Their parents died when Auntie Kathie was still in high school, so she's my only relative on my mom's side until my new cousin is born in a few months. So I'm a little startled when I don't recognize the boy about our age who answers the door. He has hooded eyes that make him look sleepy and long, skinny arms that I only notice because he's wearing one of those goofy sleeveless hoodies so that if he gets caught in the rain he can still show off his muscles. Or at least he could if he had any.

"Hey!" he says. "Are you here for the memorial?"

Memorial?

"The rest of the Guilds are inside," he says. Then his eyes widen. "Oh. Shoot. Uh, if you don't know what that is, forget I said that—"

Well, I guess now we know that Auntie Kathie was part of this, too. That's a relief, but I can't help but feel a twinge of disappointment at the same time.

Even before Auntie Kathie moved down here, when I only used to see her once a year when we went to Vegas every winter break to visit her, she'd always been my favorite auntie. She's cool, fun, and tells me the wildest stories about life in show business. Plus, she's always straight with me. My aunt's frankness makes Mom shake her head and Dad blush sometimes, but I don't like being lied to. I always respected Auntie Kathie for that. I can't believe she, of all adults, could be okay with keeping me in the dark about all of this. Whatever *this* is.

"Yeah, I know about the Guilds," I say quickly. That's only true in the sense that I know they exist, but that's enough to satisfy him. Which makes one of us.

"Okay, cool, cool," he says, obviously relieved. He holds the door open to let us inside. We put down our skateboards, take off our helmets, and step into the foyer.

I don't know how long Auntie Kathie is going to stay here after her baby is born, and it doesn't seem like she does, either. The apartment is barely furnished even though she's been living here for months. Instead of framed pictures, the hallway is decorated with Polaroids hung up with strings and clothespins.

Most of the photos are from my aunt's life in Vegas or places she visited on cruise ships, but one catches my eye. It's a selfie of my aunt and mom, sitting in an old-fashioned diner and making duck faces at the camera. Both of them are much younger: my aunt is in her homemade prom dress, and my mom was pregnant. I know it was with me, even though I've never seen this photo.

"So what Guilds are you from?" the boy asks, jolting me out of my thoughts. "I'm Kevin, by the way. Kevin Chengsson."

Uh . . . "Well, my mom's a Weaver," I say hesitantly.

"Cool, cool," says Kevin, nodding his head up and down like a bobblehead. "My mom's a Warrior."

"Warrior, nice," I say.

"Yeah, we're familiar with these concepts," Thida says drily. I elbow her, but Kevin just keeps on talking like he didn't hear her.

"She hasn't really been involved with the Guilds in a minute, though. My dad was killed by these twelve assassins called the Zodiac Killers when I was little, so she's busy hunting them down one by one to avenge his death."

He shares this information as casually as a kindergartner might recite how many siblings he has or what his parents do for a living on the first day of school. What kind of comic book gangster organization was my mom involved in?

"Uh, okay," I say, trying not to sound like I'm a normal person having a normal reaction to this news. "Uh, good for her."

"Yeah, your mom sounds cool," says Thida. My best friend always reminds me of a stone-faced gunslinger or a wandering monk in a martial arts movie.

"Thanks! So far she's taken down nine of them, so she only has Rooster, Dog, and Pig left. Are your parents Weavers, too?" Kevin asks Thida. The way he can change the subject as if he hadn't just casually said one of the most bonkers things I've ever heard makes my head spin.

"Oh, no. My mom's a urologist. That's a pee doctor," Thida explains when Kevin furrows his brow in confusion. "It's cool, though, because ninety percent of urologists are men; it's the most male-dominated field of medicine. So she's breaking down barriers in pee medicine."

Thida isn't sarcastic the way, like, characters in Marvel movies are, but the thing with her is it can be hard to tell if she's being sarcastic or not. I'm not always 100 percent sure I can tell, and we've been best friends since fourth grade. I snort, but her dry sense of humor flies right over Kevin's head.

"Oh, cool! Hey, could I ask her about something? My, uh, friend has been having this problem, and okay, it's kinda really weird—"

"Oh, hey, I see my aunt over there!" I say loudly, before he can continue that sentence. My eyes dart toward Thida, but she's right behind me. We leave Kevin standing in the foyer and dash off into the living room.

"You didn't really see your aunt, did you," Thida says once we're out of earshot.

"No." I scoff. "I just didn't need to hear about his 'friend.'" I shudder. That kid was weird. I don't even want to think about what he would consider *really* weird.

Since moving down here, Auntie Kathie has been working as an instructor for this online ballet workout class, so all of the few pieces of cute, refurbished furniture she got from the Avalon Buy Nothing group on Facebook have been pushed to the side to make room for her home studio. But today, the living room is packed with about forty Chinese people, standing around solemnly in dark button-downs and skirt suits. Everyone is very serious, which looks low-key hilarious in a room with a giant neon sign on the wall reading GOOD GIRLS GO TO HEAVEN, BAD GIRLS TO VEGAS. But now I understand what Kevin meant by this being a *memorial.* The Guilds—whoever they are—must be coming to pay their respects to my aunt after my mom's "death."

But I didn't see any of those people at *the* memorial, at my mom's actual home. Or the funeral. Why would they be visiting my aunt and not us? And if Auntie Kathie wanted to have a memorial service for my mom, why wouldn't she invite us?

With so many similarly dressed people in the small apartment, I can't see my aunt. And she's usually hard to miss, even when she isn't covered in rhinestones and feathers. My mom is above-average height for a Chinese woman, but Auntie Kathie is five foot nine, which is almost the same height as Wonder Woman. Whenever we went to Chinatown in Vegas for lunch, she always towered over every other woman around and a lot of the men, too. After I've looked around for a while and still haven't seen her, Thida starts scanning the Polaroids on the wall.

"Is that the dad?"

I jerk my head toward her. Thida is looking at a photo of Auntie Kathie in Paris, in front of the

Moulin Rouge nightclub with the red windmill on the roof. Next to her is a man with his arm around her waist and his face scribbled over in Sharpie.

"Yeah. Unfortunately." I've never met the guy, so I wouldn't be able to recognize him even if the photo was intact. But I know because the last time I was here, my mom got into an argument with my aunt about her keeping this picture up, even with his face defaced. Auntie Kathie said she'd dreamed of seeing the Moulin Rouge ever since she saw the movie when she was a kid, but Mom gets really angry at any reminder of her sister's loser ex. She won't even use his name. She just calls him "The Gambler."

Suddenly I notice two guys' heads turning toward the kitchen at the same time. Sure enough, when I look over, there's my aunt, standing by the fridge with a pint of ice cream. In contrast to the somberly dressed guests, my aunt is wearing a white slip dress that clings to her bulging belly.

Auntie Kathie sees me, too, and her mouth drops open. "Evie! What are you doing here?"

My aunt crosses the room toward me. Six months into her pregnancy, she still has her dancer's grace, but otherwise she looks like a funhouse mirror version of herself—and it's not because her belly has ballooned or her hips have gotten wider. Her hair looks like a bunch of spiders got tangled together, and though she isn't wearing any makeup, her face is red from crying.

"Hi, Auntie Kathie. I know about the Weavers," I add, and her puffy eyes open wide. "I need to show you something—"

But my aunt cuts me off. "Your mom told you about the Weavers?"

"Well, not exactly," I say, trying not to sound too touchy about my aunt's obvious surprise.

But before I can explain, Auntie Kathie grabs my wrist and pulls me toward the living room. "You have no idea how relieved the Weavers are going to be to see you."

SEVEN

ADULTS ARE (MOSTLY) USELESS

Before I can ask what she's even talking about, Auntie Kathie leads me through the crowded room and toward the small corner table where she plays poker or mahjong with my parents. Four people are seated in mismatched chairs around the table, which is covered with bouquets of white and yellow chrysanthemums. A man with aviator-style glasses and hair starting to go gray at the temples stands up to help my aunt, but she smacks his arm away playfully.

"Don't be such a simp. I'm pregnant, not old like you." Thida looks startled at my aunt's seeming rudeness to an older person, but it's nothing I haven't seen before. Mom always grumbles about how ever since they were kids, her little sister could not only get away with saying outrageous things to her elders, but they'd laugh and think it was cute. And they still do. The man doesn't even seem offended. Or maybe he does simp for my aunt. He wouldn't be the first.

Auntie Kathie turns back to me and Thida. "This is Dr. Peter Hsu, head of the Scholars, or Water Elder. Before you girls get too excited, it's a PhD."

"I flew in from Australia just for that," Dr. Hsu says drily.

Auntie Kathie sits down in an empty chair, which had been pulled out more to accommodate her belly. She sets down her ice cream, then indicates the man next to her.

"Cyrus Lie, head of the Warriors, also known as Fire Elder. Don't worry, he's only killed a few people with his bare hands. The rest were with weapons. Probably. It's hard to keep track."

Cyrus gives me a nod of acknowledgment. He's a little man, barely taller than I am, with long wavy hair tied back and light brown skin. I think my aunt is joking, but after hearing about Kevin's mom, I can't be sure.

"Metal Elder is Dr. Sylvia Fang, who *is* a medical doctor, but she's also head of the Alchemists, and they're rumored to have poisoned numerous emperors with fake elixirs for immortality. So you can decide whether or not to take your chances."

"All those accusations of being evil and power hungry are tiresome misogyny. Before the twentieth century, we were the only Guild that was open to women," explains Dr. Fang. Despite the silver streaks in her permed hair, she doesn't look much older than my mom, but something about the way she waves her hand as she scoffs reminds me of Āh Mā and her friends. "The Alchemists have never killed anyone who didn't deserve it."

"Wood Elder is Song Bo, head of the disappointments to their parents. Sorry, I meant the Artists." The final person at the table is a very old man wearing dark glasses and a black knit cap, who doesn't react at all.

"The Council are the representative heads of the five Gold Mountain Guilds." Auntie Kathie pauses, as if taking a moment to compose herself. "Your mother was Earth Elder, head of the Weavers. Now that she's passed, you'll be the new leader of our Guild." She looks around the room and announces, "Everyone, this is my niece, Evie Mei."

I have a lifetime's supply of questions right now. So my mom wasn't just head of a mystical secret society, but part of an entire *network* of secret societies? And I'm supposed to be next in line, but then *why wouldn't she tell me about this*? None of this makes any sense! Even Kevin knew about this, and he barely even sees his mom!

My face becomes hot, and I feel like when I was six and my older cousins thought it would be really funny to teach me some Chinese words at Lunar New Year, only they didn't tell me the truth about which ones. I never found out what I actually said to Āh Mā, but I knew it was bad from the way everyone around the dining table suddenly became quiet and stared at me. My mom quickly figured out what had happened and let my cousins have it, so nobody blamed me, but I still remember that awful feeling of humiliation that everyone in the room realized a joke had been played on me and I didn't. It's the same feeling now, but I remind myself that's not what matters right now. Because there is one thing I know that all the people here don't.

"Uh, yeah, about that. There's something you all should know. There's kinda been a huge misunderstanding. My mom isn't really dead."

A few Guild members exchange glances, but no one says anything. Finally, Auntie Kathie says gently, "Evie, I understand you want to believe that your mom is still out there somewhere . . ."

"It's not that! I know it." I take out the scroll from my pocket and hand it to my aunt. As she reads my mom's embroidered message—needle-writing, Monk called it—her eyes become as wide as an anime character's. By the time I've finished recapping the confrontation with Monk, my aunt's entire body is trembling.

"So Dawn has been in *Dìyù* this whole time?" Dr. Fang says incredulously. "Āiyā, she disappeared more than a week ago! Why are we only learning this now? She could be dead for real by now."

Her words feel like a kick in the stomach, but I can't let myself think about that right now. "That's why I'm here. I need your help to save her."

Dr. Fang says, "Good grief, girl, do you know what Dìyù *is*? It's not an amusement park. It's a vast subterranean maze full of all manner of horrific tortures. There's a mountain covered with long swords and pits of excrement and flaming cattle and—"

"Hey, sorry to interrupt, I know I'm just some random Burmese kid," Thida says. "But why don't we pull a Karen and try to speak to, like, the manager . . . of Hell. Or whoever's in charge down there. Evie's mom is clearly not supposed to be there, so once they see she's alive, they'll know there's been a mistake, right?"

"That's King Yama," Dr. Hsu, PhD, says. "But no, that won't work. The netherworld bureaucracy's as notoriously labyrinthine as Dìyù itself. It could take hundreds of years for anyone to even look at our complaint. But there's another way. The Staff of Mùlián."

The head of the Scholars looks at me directly as he explains, which makes me warm up to him a little. "Mùlián was a monk who successfully infiltrated Dìyù in the Tang dynasty. He claimed his great merit and religious piety allowed him to save his mother's soul, though the fact that he had a magic staff that could smash the walls of Dìyù and repel demons probably helped somewhat."

There's a magic staff that can repel demons in Dìyù?! "And where is the Staff now?" I say breathlessly.

"As it so happens, one of my art dealer contacts just recovered Mùlián's Staff from an estate sale in Pasadena. The Scholars do a lot of work investigating and tracking down artifacts of interest, many of which wound up in the grubby hands of rich Westerners thanks to colonialism. I can make a phone call and have it delivered here."

My heart is pounding so hard, it feels like it'll explode into confetti. "That's perfect! Thank you!"

The eldest Elder, Song Bo of the Artists, says something in Cantonese. Suddenly, the room goes dead silent.

"What?" I say, feeling a sense of dread as I glance around the room and am met with somber faces. Turning to Auntie Kathie, I say sheepishly, "Um, what did he say?"

"He said he just has one question," Dr. Fang says. "Who goes to Dìyù?"

"I should go, since she's my sister," Auntie Kathie starts to say, but a chorus of aunties immediately drowns her out.

"No!"

"Absolutely not!"

"What? I'm pregnant, not a potato," Auntie Kathie protests. I look at her very potato-shaped belly skeptically. Auntie Kathie sighs, "I know hungry ghosts are attracted to pregnant people, but the Staff—"

"The Staff of Mùlián repels supernatural beings. The deceased humans awaiting reincarnation in Dìyù are not ghosts, so they technically don't count as that yet," says Dr. Hsu. "Typically that wouldn't be an issue, since they have no reason to attack intruders.

But if *you* go, they might well attempt to escape Dìyù by possessing your unborn child the way that hungry ghosts would."

Okay, well, *that's* definitely a no. "It doesn't have to be you," I say, looking around the room. "We can use a spool of Weaver thread to track down Mom, and the Staff of Mùlián will keep away any demons, right? So it shouldn't be too hard."

"In theory, yes," Dr. Hsu says. "But we'd still be going into Dìyù. A place designed to be the most horrific imaginable."

Thida looks at me. "Aren't these people supposed to be, like, really powerful magicians and warriors and stuff?" she says under her breath.

"We're an association of societies dedicated to the mastery and preservation of esoteric knowledge and arcane Chinese cultural arts," replies Dr. Hsu, having apparently heard her. "Some of us are accomplished martial artists and sorcerers, and some of us are academics and make magical art. I run a museum. You'll have to forgive me if journeying to the netherworld is a little outside my area of expertise."

"That's a lot of words for 'I'm a coward,'" Auntie Kathie says snidely.

"I think everyone agrees that someone ought to

rescue Dawn," Dr. Hsu says. "I'm not trying to discourage anyone. If anyone is braver than I, by all means, go."

I look at the blank faces around the table, then toward the suddenly dead silent living room. No one speaks up, and I struggle not to scream.

"Well, don't look at me," Dr. Fang says. "I just had my hip replaced. And, ah, there might be some people in Dìyù that I would rather not see again."

"Did you send them there?" Thida asks.

Auntie Kathie sighs, but she doesn't try and argue with Dr. Fang. She doesn't look at Song Bo, either, which is fair, since he looks like he could go to sleep and wake up in Dìyù any day now. But when she glances toward Cyrus Lie, the head of the Warriors, who has been listening without saying a word throughout this entire discussion, he just shakes his head silently before she can even open her mouth.

"Seriously?" Auntie Kathie scoffs. While my aunt couldn't seem to be more different from my fussy, uptight little sister, they look alike when they pout. "The Scholars I can understand, but are the *Warriors* too chicken?"

"I'm sure that trick usually works like a charm for

you, but it won't do a thing on me," says Cyrus. "I'm very secure in my masculinity."

Despite his title, Fire Elder speaks calmly and coolly. "How can we even be sure the yāoguài is telling the truth about where Límíng"—he uses my mom's Chinese name, which also means *dawn*—"is? We should interrogate him first and uncover more information. Where did you say you left him?" he says, addressing me.

"Uh, the trash," Thida says. "We were hoping the garbage truck would take him away—oh." She winces.

"Hmm." Cyrus turns to Auntie Kathie. "The yāoguài was looking for Weaver thread to find Dawn, right? We can locate him and get him to talk, find out more about who sent him."

"But we don't have time for that," I blurt out. Looking at Dr. Fang, I continue, "You said it yourself, we don't even know if she's still alive down there." I don't want to believe that she isn't—I *can't* believe it—but it's already been ten days since she went missing. The longer we wait, the more likely she'll *die for real* down there. "We have to go get her *now*, before it's too late."

I feel like I'm going to explode. Even with a *demon-repelling staff*, not *one* of these adults will save my mom? She isn't just one of them, but one of their leaders! More than that—she's one of their *Elders*! I don't really know how that works since she's only thirty-eight years old, but still, that's supposed to be a big deal!

Suddenly I flash back to the time Thida's parents took us to the California Science Center for her birthday. There was this one-inch cable suspended forty feet in the air, like a tightrope, and a bicycle for you to *ride across*. Thida tried to convince me to try, saying that the laws of physics made it "literally impossible" to fall. But when I asked her why *she* didn't do it, then, she didn't say anything.

"Okay, you know what, *I'll* do it!" I say at last. "I'll go to Dìyù and find my mom."

Auntie Kathie says, "No, you won't."

I had been prepared to get pushback from the other Guilds, but not by my cool, fun auntie. I stare at her, feeling betrayed.

"Evie, I don't like having to be the responsible adult around here, but obviously someone has to. You are *not* going to Dìyù."

To my surprise, Dr. Hsu comes to my defense. "It

might not be as bad an idea as it sounds, you know," he muses. "The Staff doesn't require any particular training to use, so while frightening, Dìyù would be considerably less dangerous . . ."

"Then why don't *you* go?" Auntie Kathie says in disgust. When she turns back to me, her voice becomes high enough to break glass. "Look, I want her back, too. But I can't let you go into the netherworld! Even if you could bring her back without getting yourself hurt in the process, your mom would send *me* to Dìyù for letting you go after her, if you know what I mean."

"But you can't stop me! You said it yourself. Without Mom, I'm the new head of the Weavers," I say stubbornly. Even in my defiance, I know how childish I sound. Mom would be mortified if she could hear how rude I'm being to my aunt right now.

But Auntie Kathie can't help but smile. "You really mean it, huh?" she says softly. Her voice becomes wistful. "You're tough like your mom, you know."

That hits me unexpectedly hard, my eyes stinging. I blink quick and hard to dislodge tears from forming. Auntie Kathie drums her nails on the table for a while, then she says, "Well, I can't let you go to Dìyù alone, even if you do have the Staff."

She turns again to the head of the Warriors. "Fire Elder, are you sure you couldn't send one of your Warriors with her?" she pleads.

If he's bemused by her sudden change of tone, he doesn't show it. "That choice is not up to me." He clears his throat and turns to me. "Evie, I respect your courage, but war is about foresight and planning, not bravery. I cannot in good conscience send any of my Warriors into Dìyù when I don't know what horrors they might face down there, even with the Staff."

Despite his cool assessment of the situation, his tone is surprisingly kind. Still, my heart sinks. But then he adds, "However, I will not interfere if any Warrior volunteers."

He turns toward the living room, at all the people who had come to honor my mom's life but won't do anything to save it. Auntie Kathie looks like she might burst into tears again. But then, to my surprise, I see someone has raised their hand. Arm high and straight in the air, like a try-hard. My spirits rise at the sight . . . until I see whose hand it is.

"Hey, I'm Kevin Chengsson. I'll go to Dìyù with her." Kevin Chengsson smiles at me, then looks at Auntie Kathie.

My aunt opens her mouth, then closes it. "That's very sweet, Kevin. But . . ."

Kevin adds, "In exchange, I just want to know who my red string of fate is tied to."

I have no idea what that is, but judging by the snickers that go around the room, I'm not sure I want to find out. I start to panic, but I tell myself I'm being too quick to judge. After all, this kid grew up in the Warriors, which is more than I can say about the Weavers.

But Cyrus Lie looks just as skeptical, to my dismay. "Kevin, I see you have your mother's, ah, bravery," he says, though his pause suggests there's another word he's thinking of. "But I'm not sure you're ready—"

"Nuh-uh! You just said you wouldn't stop *any* Warrior from volunteering," Kevin says triumphantly. I want to slap my forehead, but he's right, and the head of the Warriors seems to realize it.

"Hmm. I guess I did." Cyrus seems a little amused to admit defeat. Auntie Kathie looks at him with disbelief, but he sighs and throws his hands up in the air. "What can I say? I'm a man of my word."

Thida shoots me a sideways look, as if to say *Really?* But honestly? The fact that I have no better options just makes me even more determined. And anyway, I have Mom's string and the Staff of Mùlián, too. It's just like the bicycle and the wire, right? No one wants to do it because it *looks* really scary, but I'll be safe with the Staff. If I really had to, I'd go into Dìyù alone and armed with a pool noodle to save Mom.

I nod at my aunt, who looks like she's about to throw up. She looks at me and then at Kevin, but seeing his eager nod, she purses her lips. "All right, hun," she says. I think she's trying to put on her showgirl smile, I guess to be nice. But by now I can recognize instantly when someone isn't smiling with their eyes. "You've got yourself a deal."

"Sweet!" Kevin shoots his stupid sleeveless arms up into the air, while I try not to think too hard about what I've gotten myself into.

EIGHT

THE SECRET HISTORY OF SECRET SOCIETIES

As soon as Dr. Hsu has called his dealer, most of the Guild members aside from the Elders and Kevin Chengsson take off. I guess they were here to pay their respects to Mom, so there's no reason for them to stick around now that she's not dead. But they all insist on personally saying goodbye to me and wishing me good luck saving my mom from the netherworld. I'd have preferred actual help from more of these magical adults, but that's nice of them.

But then Dr. Hsu steps back into the room and tells me to clear all the flowers from the table, and I see that Song Bo, the head of the Artists, has taken out a brush, a pot of ink, and an engraved black disk with a circle in the center.

"Mùlián had to travel to Mount Tai in China to

find the entrance to Dìyù, but Wood Elder is a master of landscape traveling," Dr. Hsu explains. "It's a technique created by the great Tang painter Wu Daozi. He can paint a scene and the painting becomes a portal to that location."

I'm still feeling a little salty, but it's a huge relief that I just have to wait for him to finish one painting instead of having to fly all the way to China. While we wait for the Staff of Mùlián and for Wood Elder to finish, I decide to talk to my aunt. I was prepared to wait to rescue my mom first, but there's still so much I need to know about her double life. But when I look around, my aunt has disappeared.

I turn to Kevin Chengsson. (At first I thought I had misheard his name and it was something like "Kevin Cheng Sun," but no, he definitely pronounces it like one word, "Chengsson." That baffles me—did his ancestors think slapping a "son" at the end of their name would make the racists think they're not Chinese or something?)

"Hey," I say. "Have you seen my aunt?"

"Oh yeah," Kevin replies. "She said she was gonna have the Elders burn some money for us to take to Dìyù."

"She's going to what now?" Thida says.

But for once, I know exactly what Kevin is talking about. During Mom's funeral, we burned piles of fake money printed out of joss paper, which Āh Mā explained is for the dead to use in the afterlife. I don't really understand what use money would be in Dìyù, though. Is there an infernal convenience store where the dead can buy Band-Aids for their torture wounds?

"Hey, uh, thanks for volunteering," I say to Kevin, trying to sound thankful. It seems to work as Kevin's face lights up.

"The Warriors are always saying I'm 'completely hopeless,' but guess what? None of them volunteered and I did."

He reaches into the pocket of his black hoodie tank and pulls out a butterfly knife. He tries to flip it open but misses, and it falls to the ground.

"Well," Thida says as he bends to pick it up and I try not to lose my mind. "It's a good thing you'll have the Staff."

Auntie Kathie emerges from her bedroom then, carrying two red boxes. Though her eyes are still puffy, she seems calmer now. Mom is like that, too—having something useful that she can do calms her down. "We're going to burn this for you. It's supposed to materialize on the other side, so you should be able to access it once you're in Dìyù."

She shows us a box filled with joss paper dollars. Each note reads BANK OF HEAVEN AND EARTH and TEN THOUSAND DOLLARS and is printed with the image of a demonic-looking Chinese emperor.

"Āh Mā said burning these is tradition, but what would the dead even have to buy in Dìyù?" I ask.

"I have no idea, but before your great-grandparents immigrated to America, my grandfather's auntie told him: 'Remember, my son: No matter where you go, everyone loves money.'" Auntie Kathie smirks. "I always thought it was hilarious that she didn't tell him to work hard or to make his parents proud or your typical Asian auntie wisdom—she told him *that*. Let's see whether that includes Dìyù, too."

She shows me the second box, which has a picture of a paper smartphone, a credit card, and a designer handbag. "I'll have them burn the phone, too. I don't know if the reception will be any good in the netherworld, but maybe you can use the flashlight."

"You burn phones and credit cards for the dead, too?" Thida asks.

"Some people even burn paper cars and houses. Who knows if they get to keep them, though." Auntie

Kathie sighs. "I only bought this because it came as a bargain. I'll have them burn the bag, too, so you can have something to put things in."

"Can I talk to you for a bit?" I say as my aunt turns to go. "I only learned about all of . . . this from the monkey, so I still don't really understand any of it."

"Of course. I was just going to give these to the Elders. I can't be around it once it burns because the smoke isn't good for pregnant people. I'll be right back. You can wait for me in my bedroom and I'll talk to you in private." To Thida, she says, "No offense, hun. Trade secrets."

She turns to go, but pauses and looks at the wall. After hesitating for a moment, she yanks off the Polaroid of her and her faceless ex in front of the Moulin Rouge, then slips it under the paper money.

"Is she gonna send her ex to Dìyù, too?" Thida whispers to me.

"I heard that!" Auntie Kathie calls over her shoulder. "It doesn't work like that. There's a process that goes into making spirit offerings. I'm just throwing out some trash."

She leaves with the money and the photo. My mom would be proud of her, but it makes me kind of sad that she finally got to see Paris and some jerk ruined it for her.

I leave Thida with Kevin in the living room, which is sure to be an interesting conversation, and head to my aunt's bedroom. A crib that looks like a giant sewing basket sits at the foot of the bed; the hot-pink makeup bag where Auntie Kathie keeps her actual sewing supplies sits on her bedside table along with her Polaroid camera. Instead of Polaroids, she's put up stickers of stars and cute animals. Also hanging up on the wall is at what first glance looks like a large painting of lovers embracing in a starry sky, standing on a bridge of black-and-white magpies. But after it hits me why the scene looks so familiar—it's the same composition on the cover of my mom's thread book—I realize the "painting" is actually embroidery, with superthin threads imitating the style of a traditional Chinese ink painting. There's even calligraphy text accompanying the image, done in black stitches.

"My great-grandpa made that," Auntie Kathie announces as she enters the room. In her hands are two pints of red bean ice cream. "It's the Cowherd and the Weaver Girl. Did your mom tell you that story?"

Auntie Kathie offers me a pint of ice cream along with a plastic spoon. I've never eaten ice cream straight from the carton before, and I have to admit, it makes me feel pretty powerful. I sit down on the bed, allowing my aunt to sit in the comfy-looking purple velvet chair.

"Yeah, all the time. That's the Chinese Valentine's Day story, right?" The Weaver Girl was the daughter of the Queen of Heaven, and one day she and her sisters came to Earth to bathe in a lake. The Cowherd came along and stole her clothes, and when she saw they were missing and was freaking out because she couldn't go back to Heaven without them, guess who came along saying, *Don't worry, I have found your clothes!* And she went, *My hero!!* Kind of a creepy thing to do, but I guess it worked because they fell in love and got married. But the Queen of Heaven was upset because her daughter had abandoned her heavenly weaving duties. So the Weaver Girl's mother dragged her back to Heaven, even though she and the Cowherd had already started a family. In the end, they were allowed to reunite once every year on a bridge of magpies.

Auntie Kathie nods. "According to family lore, we're descended from their half-mortal children."

"So we're, like, part god?"

"After thousands of years and who knows how many generations? No more than a tiny fraction of a percent, which is probably about the same as any average person off the street. But the Weaver Girl did leave her spindle from Heaven—the Spindle of Fate—with her son. He was the first Weaver. He had learned from his mother how to weave all kinds of magical string, which he taught to many students. The rest of the Weavers are their descendants, whether by blood or apprenticeship. But he taught only his own son how to weave threads of fate. If your mother had died before she could pass the secret down, it's not just Dawn who would have been lost. Our family's most precious magic would die out, too."

I guess that's why my aunt said the Weavers would be relieved to see me, not realizing that Mom didn't actually pass on the family secret to me yet. I don't care about saving our family's magic from dying out nearly as much as I care about getting my mom back, but that does remind me.

"But that's what I don't understand. The Weavers are like . . . a family business, right? If I'm supposed to take over the Weavers someday, why didn't she tell me about them?" I try not to sound angry, but I can't help it.

Auntie Kathie's voice becomes firm, but her eyes are filled with understanding. "Oh, your mom had a reason. You can decide whether or not it's a good one, but it was a reason."

That . . . does not make me feel good about what I'm about to hear. But okay, let's hear it.

"According to tradition, the Spindle of Fate was always passed down not from father to child, but father to *son*. It's not just sexism—"

"How is that not sexism? That's literally sexism."

"Well, yes, obviously, but please let me finish, Evie." Auntie Kathie sounds a little impatient, just like Mom did—does when I interrupt her.

"Traditionally Chinese families believed that since girls would go to live with their husbands' families after they married, they were really part of their future husbands' families as much as, if not more than, their birth family. So if a daughter inherited the Spindle, it'd be like the secret would go to another family."

I force myself not to say anything, but I have to fight the impulse pretty hard. What the heck is that all about?

"Now, of course your grandpa didn't have any sons. That didn't bother him too much because he was so proud of your mom and he wanted to pass the Spindle to her. But even though a lot of traditions had changed by the time your mom and I were growing up, the Spindle of Fate was still seen as so important that he couldn't allow the secret to leave the family. So he decided that in order for him to teach your mom, she had to swear she would never tell the man she married about the Spindle.

"At first it wasn't that hard for her to keep Guilds business a secret from him—your dad's Chinese is pretty bad, so she could bring him along to parties with other Guild members and he wouldn't understand what anyone was talking about anyway." That freaks me out a little bit—did my mom talk about Weaver business right in front of *me* and I had no idea? "But then you were born, and she realized that if she couldn't tell your dad, she also couldn't tell you or your sister until you were old enough to be trusted not to blurt it out to him."

"But that doesn't make any sense," I say, my face getting hot. "I'm still a Huang, too, even if my dad doesn't know about the Spindle. What difference does it make?"

"I think your grandfather was really worried about a divorce. It was the nineties, Princess Diana and Prince Charles had just gotten divorced and that was a whole thing . . . But of course it doesn't make any sense," Auntie Kathie says, before I can ask how the heck

Princess Diana getting divorced means I couldn't be told the truth about our family. "Traditionally, he would have had to adopt a boy just to have a son to pass his knowledge to. But your grandfather wasn't some evil girl-hating dinosaur, either. He would have been going against our family's rules for centuries, and he felt like this was the compromise he had to make in order to break against tradition. That doesn't mean your mom felt okay about lying to your dad. But she had made a promise to your grandpa, and your mom does *not* break her promises."

I can't argue with that: Mom *always* keeps her promises. But I can't understand how my proud, fiercely independent mother could ever have agreed to make such an unfair promise in the first place. This is a woman who once made Mona Li and me literally sign contracts swearing we'll never marry a guy who won't do his fair share of chores.

I take a deep breath, letting my most important question rise to the surface among all this information. "But if she didn't tell me before because I was too young to keep it a secret from my dad, why did you sound so surprised when you thought Mom had told me?"

Auntie Kathie takes a while to answer. "I didn't

want to be the one to tell you this, but I guess it can't be helped now. Since there's only one Spindle, only one child each generation is taught to use it. When you showed up here asking about the Weavers, I'd assumed your mom must have changed her mind, but . . . from what I understood, she was planning to pass the secret to your sister."

I'd expected some infuriating answer about how they *had* to lie to me to protect me or whatever. But I was *not* expecting this.

I don't blame Mom for deciding to teach Mona Li over me. I don't. She was always way more interested in following Mom's footsteps. I always said my sister could have the shop, and it'd be pretty stupid to get jealous of something that I didn't even want anyway. But now I have to wonder: Was Mom just never going to tell me at all?

"But if the Spindle is so powerful, why doesn't Mom just change her fate so she's back on Earth?" I say, suddenly desperate to change the subject. From Auntie Kathie's quick release of breath, I think she feels the same way.

"Two reasons. First, the Spindle of Fate can *alter* fate, but it can't *control* it. Everyone is born with multiple invisible threads of fate that are woven before we're born. These are all the circumstances in our lives that are beyond our control: who your parents are, whether they're rich or poor, chance meetings or freak accidents, who we love.

"What makes the Spindle of Fate so special is that it can weave *new* threads. All other circumstances in a person's life could be leading toward them becoming a doctor, but the Spindle could weave them a string of fate so that they are fated to become a rock star instead. Once woven, this thread will be inevitable, though exactly how it fits in the larger fabric of that person's life is completely beyond the Weaver's control. Each individual thread is only that: one strand out of countless interwoven threads. Fate is like a tapestry: You don't get the entire picture just by looking at each individual thread in turn. But also, people aren't tapestries. We can change some of the circumstances in our lives with our efforts and our choices, for one. And for another, our threads are also connected to and entangled with each other's."

"But couldn't my mom just weave more threads?"

Auntie Kathie smirks. "Not to sound like a boomer, but that question is why there are barely any Weavers left. Most of the ancient traditions that the Guilds are dedicated to cultivating are very hard to learn, which is why we need to preserve them. Most Guild members devote their entire lives to the mastery of a single skill. Weaver magic is very powerful, but it's also slow. You don't just say some words and control fate. It'd take your mom many hours of spinning and intense mental concentration to produce even a single thread."

Before it was impossible for me to wrap my head around my mom—who organizes her closet by material and is obsessed with Costco—as magical. But now I have to admit, this sounds like the perfect kind of magic for her: one all about hard work and painstaking attention to detail. *Of course* that's the kind of magic she would have.

"What's the second reason?"

"The Spindle of Fate has only one weakness, but it's a big one. You can't use it to change your own fate."

I remember what Mom said about getting her fortune told: If she could change her fate, she'd do it on her own, but if she couldn't, then there was no point worrying about it. That all sounded sensible enough, but I wonder now if Mom wasn't more afraid to know her own fate than she had let on. How must that feel, to be able to change everyone else's destiny but not your own?

I still have so many questions, but suddenly the doorbell rings. The Staff of Mùlián is here. I can't waste any more time lounging around in my aunt's apartment talking about the past. Not while Mom is trapped in Dìyù.

Auntie Kathie takes both of our pints of ice cream and sets them down on her bedside table, then hugs me. "I think you'll be just fine," she says brightly. "You'll have the Staff of Mùlián, and more importantly, you've got your mom's spirit."

At first I think she means I have my mom's iron will and determination inside me, too. But then she reaches out and taps my red string pendant, and I remember that Monk said it was a protective talisman. I guess it can only be so powerful, since Mom has one and she was still kidnapped by a yāoguài. But even if it's just a little bit of security, knowing that my mom is somehow still protecting me even while she's lost in Dìyù makes me feel a surge of warmth inside.

As my aunt looks at the talisman, she suddenly curses. "Oh, I completely forgot . . . After your mom inherited the Spindle of Fate, your grandpa restrung her talisman with additional protections so it would resist magical attempts to locate her. Otherwise she'd be bombarded by all sorts of beings trying to change their fates. I don't know how the yāoguài managed to find her, but he must have used non-magical means, otherwise the talisman would have thrown him off."

It takes a moment for me to realize what my aunt's suggesting. "Does that mean Weaver thread wouldn't be able to find her, either? Because of her talisman?"

Auntie Kathie nods. "That's why the Weavers couldn't use a spool to find her body after we thought she'd drowned."

My heart sinks, but then my aunt walks over to her hot-pink makeup bag. She unzips it and plucks out a spool of red thread. "Since this is a family spool, it can counteract the talisman a little bit. Your mom's talisman is stronger, so the thread will eventually start tangling when you get closer to her. But at least you'll know you're headed in the right direction instead of having to fumble your way all over Dìyù."

I guess Monk didn't know that. Or did he? "What if I used the string of the talisman my mom made for me?" I ask, and my hand immediately reaches up for it. "Would it be strong enough to take me all the way to Mom?"

Auntie Kathie hesitates. "Your mother made it for her own child, so it probably would be able to find her just fine. But I don't think that's a good idea. You'd have to untie the knots, and that would mean dropping your mother's protection over you."

My aunt suddenly becomes very quiet. Though she doesn't say it, I'm pretty sure she's thinking that I will need all the protection I can get in Dìyù. "Are you making a talisman for your baby?" I say after a while, trying to lighten the mood.

Auntie Kathie nods. Instinctively, her hand goes to the red string around her own neck. "I'm almost done, so I just have to decide on a name. Right now I'm thinking Elvira or Keanu."

I think those are the best names I've ever heard. My aunt opens the door, but then stops to hand me back my ice cream, as well as to swipe something off her dresser.

"Don't think I forgot," she says, winking as she hands me a red envelope. She shuffles out of the room to answer the doorbell, and I head back to the living room.

"Where's Kevin?" I ask Thida. I join my best friend on the shiny love seat sofa, which is as pink as a lawn flamingo.

"He went to use the bathroom." Thida shudders,

and I decide not to ask. She shakes her head. "He showed me this poem he wrote called 'Soulmates.' He rhymed 'females' with 'emails.'"

I think I can hear Shakespeare's ghost screaming. I decide to drop the subject.

"So, I was thinking, if we go to Dìyù, we might be gone a while," I say. "My dad has a lot to do today, so he probably won't worry for at least a few hours, but if we're out longer than that, he'll probably try and text you." I can't believe I'm about to ask this. Even though it lasted only about two seconds, the moment when Dad briefly let his smiling mask slip is burned into my mind. The last thing he needs is to worry about me, too. "Could you stay here so you can talk to him if he gets worried?"

Thida looks at me, surprised. "Can't your aunt do that?"

"No, I didn't tell him we were going to see Auntie Kathie and I'm not gonna. If he knows I came over here, he might stop by to pick us up since it's so close."

Thida makes a face like she bit into a lemon. "That's . . . responsible of you. What happened to my best friend?"

I almost ask what that's supposed to mean, but I've

stayed up too many school nights watching R-rated movies while my parents were asleep to act like I don't already know.

"I thought my mom died is what happened. Kinda had to step up after that."

"Well, it's a good thing she's really alive, because it's freaking me out." Thida's eyes dart to the hallway, her lips pursed. "It's just . . . I mean, *that* kid, really?" She groans. "Why couldn't his mom go with you to the netherworld?"

"Okay, maybe we should give him a chance," I push back. "I mean, okay yeah, he's kind of a doofus, and yeah, all the Warriors laughed when he volunteered . . ." My fingers twitch with anxiety, and I remind myself I'm supposed to be convincing Thida. "But he was the only one who was brave enough to volunteer at all. That has to count for something."

"Maybe he's brave, or maybe he's a dumb boy trying to prove he's tougher than he is." I wince, because as harsh as Thida's words are, she's probably not wrong. I flash back to when we were helping Auntie Kathie move into her new apartment and my dad kept insisting that her various pieces of furniture were "not heavy, just awkward," only to end up throwing out his back.

"Okay, you might be right. But no offense, would you really be any better? You run a twelve-minute mile."

Thida glares at me, but I stare back, holding eye contact. I break and start laughing first because I can never win a stare down with Thida. But then she sighs, and I know I've rested my case.

"Okay. I'll stay here. But try to call or text me when you get to Dìyù." She takes out her Sharpie from her backpack and writes her phone number on my arm.

"I will. Or at least, I'll try. The reception probably sucks in the netherworld." When Thida's finished writing, I ask, "Can I borrow your phone for a second?"

Thida takes out her phone, enters the passcode, and hands it over. I start typing a message: *Robin to Batman. I'm going to sleep over at Thida's house*, but then I think it over and realize Dad might call Thida's parents and find out I'm not there. So I delete the last part and type, *Going to get boba with Thida. Might sleep over* instead. Hopefully it won't take that long to find Mom with the string and the Staff, but I don't want my dad to be too worried if it does. I add a heart emoji, then hit send.

"If my dad calls you, tell him we're getting boba," I say as I hand Thida back her phone.

Thida nods. "You probably should use the bathroom, too."

"Good idea." I go take care of that. When I come back out, Auntie Kathie is in the living room, holding the spool of red thread.

"The Elders are in the front," she says. She takes the thread around the spool and ties it around my index finger. "Just tell the spool where you need to go, and it'll take care of the rest. Once you start getting close to her, the thread will start to tangle. But you'll know you're on the right track."

Auntie Kathie also hands me back Mom's scroll. "Keep that with you. If I need to communicate with you and you can't get reception, I'll sew you a message."

Nodding, I stuff the scroll back in my pocket. Then I follow Auntie Kathie to the front door, where the Elders and Kevin are gathered. Dr. Hsu is carrying a wooden staff topped with interconnected metal rings. Before I can take it from him, Song Bo hands me his finished painting. The ink looks dry, but the paper is thin and delicate, so I take it carefully.

"This is Dìyù?" I say. His style is more abstract and energetic than my great-great-grandfather's meticulously detailed needlework "painting," with relatively few brushstrokes creating surprisingly vivid images. But the picture itself reminds me of a creepy drawing that a disturbed child might create in a horror movie, if he also happened to be really talented. It's not a "landscape" so much as a collection of random, violent scenes, showing people with anguished faces being chased by snarling demons with farming implements, cooked in a giant cauldron of oil, and forced to climb a mountain covered with swords.

"He drew on historical and literary descriptions of the torments of Dìyù, but the place may have changed after hundreds of years, so this might not be a hundred percent accurate," Dr. Hsu says delicately. "That shouldn't affect your ability to enter, however. According to Wood Elder, landscape travel is really more about capturing the essence of a place than perfect verisimilitude."

As frustrated as I was with the Elders for being too chicken to go to Dìyù, I have to admit that's really cool. "Thank you. It's, uh, beautiful."

Dr. Sylvia Fang steps forward next. She walks with the support of a cane, along with a young woman holding on to her arm. Dr. Fang hands me and Kevin each a grain of rice. Just one.

"Swallow that and it'll expand inside your stomach, so you won't get hungry in Dìyù. The Alchemists developed this to solve food insecurity, but it causes your stomach to explode if you eat it regularly, so it's not good for long-term use."

I almost ask how she knows that, but then decide I don't really want to know the answer. Dr. Fang is definitely at least a little bit evil, but just a little bit. I think. Not getting hungry in Dìyù would come in handy, though. The food is probably terrible in Hell. I swallow the grain of rice and thank her, too. She beams.

Cyrus Lie doesn't give us anything. He just tells Kevin, "Remember what I told you."

Dr. Hsu hands the Staff of Mùlián to Kevin. "So how do I use this thing?" he asks.

"All you have to do is shake it. The ringing sound will drive away any demons you encounter. It can also knock down Dìyù's walls."

I think that's the last of it, but then Thida steps forward and hands me my shoes and helmet.

"Oh, right. I really don't know what I'd do without you sometimes," I say as I put them on. I try to say it lightheartedly, but it comes out a little more panicked than I intended.

"I really don't know, either," Thida says. Then she hugs me.

"You don't have to do that, you know," I say. "Since my mom is alive."

"Okay, good. It's so awkward," Thida says. I laugh, but even though I told her to stay to reassure my dad, the truth is I would feel a lot better if my best friend were going with me.

Song Bo hands me another painting, this one of a room. It's also in black ink, but with a single spot of color in the form of a bright pink couch. I realize this is Auntie Kathie's living room. "Make sure you don't lose this one. That's your way back," says Dr. Hsu. Kevin takes it, and my throat goes dry as I flash back to him dropping the butterfly knife, but then he unzips his hoodie and reveals an inside pocket, which he slips it into before zipping the hoodie back up.

"Now for your way in," says Dr. Hsu. Swallowing, I hold up the ink landscape of Dìyù. Song Bo says some words, and Dr. Hsu translates, "Focus on the painting. Clear your mind and let it wander through the landscape. Eventually you'll feel your mind drifting into the scene, but don't take your eyes off the painting. This is the only dangerous part—if you break concentration too early, the transition just won't work, but if you look away while you're already in the process of traveling inside, your consciousness could be split so your body remains here while your mind is inside the landscape, which in this case is the netherworld."

My stomach lurches. "How do we know when it's safe to look away?"

Song Bo explains, and Dr. Hsu translates, "You should be able to feel once you're in a new location—from a change in temperature or light, or hearing new sounds, though Wood Elder would advise you take a deep breath and count to twenty before looking around. Since there's two of you, that'll make it easier—you can confer with each other first, just keep your eyes on the painting as you do so."

On that last note, Kevin looks at me. "You ready?"

I remind myself how much faith my mom had in me. *I know you can do it if you work hard.*

"Yeah."

I fix my eyes right on the painting, and the room goes silent as I mentally trace every ink line and brushstroke. I feel a jolt as I take in every detail of Song Bo's depiction of Dìyù. Even with his more abstract style, the hellish imagery sends a shiver up my spine, but I force myself to not look away . . .

NINE

WELCOME TO DÌYÙ! EVERYTHING IS (NOT) FINE

I keep staring at the painting, but instead of my vision blurring, it seems to become more vivid, until the image of the netherworld seems to blot out everything else. Remembering Dr. Hsu's warning, I keep my eyes on the painting even as I start to become lightheaded, until suddenly I can't see—or feel—the paper between my fingers anymore.

For a terrifying moment, I think I lost my concentration. Like whenever Mom tried to teach me to sew or make knotted charms and my mind ended up splitting from my body, and that's why I can't see anything. My chest becomes tight, like when I finally fall asleep only to dream I'm drowning and I can't move my arms and legs. But then I remember that Dìyù is supposed to be really dark. I also realize I'm freezing.

"Did we make it?" At the sound of Kevin's voice near me in the darkness, echoing like we're in a cave, I feel a rush of relief. But I remember what Song Bo recommended.

"I think so, but count to twenty?" I take a deep breath, then do exactly that. By the time I'm done, it's still cold and pitch black, so dark that it somehow hurts my eyes, like a too-bright light would.

"Uh," I say as I realize that even if I were to look around, I wouldn't be able to see anything. My hands are no longer holding the painting of Dìyù, though—does that mean we've gone through it? "I think so, but . . . now what?"

Oh! The phone! I fumble to unbutton my shorts pockets—my mom always sews pockets with buttons—and feel what seems like a stack of dollar bills and a three-dimensional smartphone. Relieved, I fish out the phone and am feeling around for the side button when a flash of green light appears. I look toward it and see that Kevin has pulled out a laser pointer that emits a thin beam, like a pocket-sized lightsaber. The laser is too thin to work as a flashlight, but it gives me just enough light to turn on the phone. And if we lose the Staff of Mùlián, we can distract the demons like cats.

The screen lights up, and I quickly press and hold the flashlight icon. When the light appears, it feels like coming up for air, even though it's still very dark and I can't see anything more than five feet away from me. Standing almost shoulder to shoulder with me is Kevin, holding the laser pointer and the Staff of Mùlián as well as a designer handbag. High above my head and jutting from the ground are pointed rock formations, like rows of jagged teeth. Speaking of which, my own teeth are chattering.

"I thought Hell was supposed to be hot," I mutter, running my hands up and down my bare arms. My tank top and shorts were perfectly appropriate for the middle of summer, but now my arms and legs are miserable. "It's like fifty degrees here."

"You've never been outside of California, huh?" Kevin grins, even though he must be freezing, too. "Do you want my jacket?"

"It's okay, thanks." His "jacket" is basically just half a layer anyway.

"Are you sure? You seem really cold."

I try to reply but can't because my teeth are chattering, even though we've been here for barely two minutes. "Won't you be cold, then? You were wearing a jacket back in my aunt's house when it was almost a hundred degrees outside."

"I'll live. I'm part Icelandic! And I just wore this because I don't have any clean black shirts." Huh, I guess there *is* a specific situation in which you would need an outer layer but your arms would be too hot. "We can take turns, though, if you feel bad."

I did feel bad, but I really am freezing. And that does make me feel a little better, so I say, "Okay. Thanks."

Kevin takes off his hoodie, revealing a basketball jersey. The Lakers, not the Warriors. He hands the "jacket" to me and I put it on. Just as I figured, it's not really that great since it doesn't do anything to warm my arms, and it's also a bit big since Kevin is taller than me, meaning there's some empty space between my upper body and the jacket. But it's better than just a tank top.

I hold out my other hand with the spool tied to my index finger. "Take me to Mom," I say, then let the spool fall like a yo-yo. As soon as it hits the ground, it starts to unravel, rolling off into the darkness.

"Here I come, Mom," I murmur, and start walking in the direction of the thread. Kevin holds on to the Staff like a walking stick and follows.

After we've walked about twenty steps, I finally get a better look at what it is we're walking toward. Ahead of us is an imposing black gate with two big yellow blobs on either side like the stone lions in front of temples in Chinatown. When I raise my phone, I can make out a horizontal plaque nailed over the arch. Characters are written across in fluorescent paint, so I can read it—well, I could if I could read Chinese.

每个人都会犯错,
有些人会比别人犯得更多

I can understand a little Chinese from listening to my mom talk with customers and older relatives, but my dad had to go to Chinese school when he was a kid and hated it so much that he refused to send me or Mona Li there. Mom tried to teach me to read and write herself when I was little, but it's a lot harder to learn than English since every word is a different character instead of based on an alphabet, and she never had enough time with the shop, so she eventually dropped it. Sheepishly, I turn to Kevin. "Do you know what that says?"

"Yeah. It means 'Everyone makes mistakes. Some more than others.'"

"Wow. That's poetry." As we get closer to the gate, I can see that the blobs are actually two enormous security guards in fluorescent-yellow boiler suits that make them look like the world's most overpowered crossing guards.

I remind myself not to be intimidated. Even if they try to throw us out, we could bring the entire gate down onto their heads with the Staff of Mùlián. But maybe we don't have to do that. Remembering what Auntie Kathie told me, I open the purse and take out a netherworld bank note.

"Uh, hi," I say as we approach the gate. "Um, I—we'd like to go into Dìyù . . ."

I wave a ten-thousand-dollar bill, which is as crisp as the ones my parents get from the bank right before Lunar New Year for red envelope money. Right in front of the gate, the fluorescent characters shine light onto the guards, and the sight nearly makes me drop the phone. From the neck down, they're humanoid, though unnaturally tall and jacked humans. But the one on the left has the face of a horse, while the one on the right has the head of an ox. Both have glowing eyes like hot coals and brandish nasty-looking weapons: Ox-Head has a three-pronged spear similar to a trident, while Horse-Face has a metal club with protruding spikes.

Ox-Head and Horse-Face peer at the ten-thousand-dollar bill in my hands, then exchange glances.

"Huh. That's the first time anyone's offered us money to get *into* Dìyù." My relief that they can speak English quickly wears off as Ox-Head literally looks down at us, sizing us up. The netherworld guards stand almost eight feet tall and are nearly as wide across the chest, and I try not to tremble as he looks us over with his coal-like cow eyes. "Wait. Is that—that's Mùlián's Staff. How'd you kids get ahold of it?"

"Are you his descendants? I guess the whole monk thing didn't work out, huh?" Horse-Face bursts out into a high whinnying laugh. "Which of your ancestors ended up in Dìyù this time?"

Ox-Head says, "I'll tell you what. I'll let you in for another ten thousand bucks."

"Hey, wait," I say as he reaches for the bank note in my hand. "You just said you don't need money to let people in. So why should I give you *more* money?"

"I said we don't normally take money to let people *in*," Ox-Head says, emphasizing the last word. It takes a moment for his meaning to sink in, and when it does I'm horrified. So that's what we burn funeral money for? So our loved ones can pay off the greedy afterlife guards? "Or you could wave Mùlián's Staff at us and get in for free, but then we would alert King Yama."

"Or, how about you just take the note I already offered you, and you don't have to worry about me telling your boss that you're taking bribes—"

"Just give it to him, we have more," Kevin pipes up. I glare at him, speechless, as Ox-Head's eyes light up like a neon sign. I can practically hear the *Ka-ching!* going off in his ox-head.

"And I suppose you could just wave the Staff at Yama, too. But every extra moment you have to deal with one of us is another that whoever you've come down here for is suffering unspeakable torment in Dìyù . . . or you could just hand over another ten thousand dollars."

He holds out an eerily human hand. I stare at it, disgusted and unable to shake the feeling that I'm being ripped off. My mom raised me to know a bad deal when I saw one. She even reads all the terms and conditions before she lets us download anything, which Thida said she thought only psychopaths did. But just like I used to tell Mom when she'd take me to Chinatown and she'd spend twenty minutes haggling, we don't have all day. If Mom gets killed by a yāoguài or a flaming cow or whatever down here, she could be stuck here forever.

Reluctantly, I fork over the ten thousand dollars, then ten thousand more. I guess my great-grandpa's auntie was right about money. It makes me want to throw up.

"Sweet!" Kevin says. He steps forward, but Horse-Face blocks his path with his spiked club.

"*Each*," he says, coal eyes twinkling. Glaring at Kevin, I hand over two more ten-thousand-dollar notes.

Smirking, Horse-Face raises his weapon. Ox-Head takes a step backward and grabs the brass knocker on the massive black gate. As he pulls the doors open, the spool suddenly starts moving again, rolling straight through the entrance. Even though I still feel like a chump, I steel myself: Mom is waiting for me. Taking a deep breath, I step inside, Kevin following with the Staff.

"You just had to tell them we have *more money*, huh?" I say through gritted teeth as we walk past the gate.

Kevin looks taken aback, like he only just noticed that I'm mad at him. If King Yama ever finds out Ox-Head and Horse-Face are taking bribes, he should put Kevin Chengsson in charge of guarding Dìyù instead, because nothing is going to get past him. "Hey, it's not so bad," he says. "I mean, it's not like you could even use the money anyway."

"That's not the point!" That I have to say that annoys me even more, like he thinks I'm not only so selfish to care about money when my mom's life is on the line, but that I'm so dumb I don't realize it's fake money. "Those guys had nothing on us and totally knew it, and you just told them we're desperate."

"But isn't that why your aunt gave you that money in the first place? So what's the point of fighting with them about it?"

I flash back to all the times Mom asked me why I have to be so argumentative. "Whatever," I mutter.

The doors slam shut behind us, and I look around Dìyù.

Even though we seem to be indoors now, it's still dark, with the only light coming from some video screens. Dozens, if not hundreds, of people sit on the floor or pace aimlessly up and down the vast space. Everyone is dressed identically in white sweatsuits made of a thin, itchy-looking material, with no socks or shoes on their feet. That makes me uneasy, because we're obviously not supposed to be here, but no one seems to pay us any attention. I guess if I had died and gone to the "bad place," I would have bigger things to worry about than some random kids walking around.

It hits me then that we're surrounded by dead people. Suddenly I feel queasy. I'm not scared of the people around us, not really—like Dr. Hsu said, they don't have any reason to bother us. It's more like the feeling I get when I go to the supermarket and see the live fish and crabs and lobsters crammed together in the tanks, knowing they're all going to be someone's lunch or dinner soon. The people around me don't look any different from normal people—they're not see-through like ghosts or rotting like zombies. But that makes it even more unsettling somehow, to be standing in a room full of people and knowing that almost everyone else in the crowd is dead . . . and doomed.

But there's only one person I have to worry about right now. My eyes track the spool as it rolls across the floor. As we push our way through the room, the spool continues to unravel at a steady pace without tangling, meaning Mom probably isn't in the First Court. That's disappointing, not just because I'm impatient to find her, but because that kills any hope that Mom might have been able to blend in with the dead here and avoid any of the truly scary stuff that the Guilds were so afraid of encountering in Dìyù.

We pass several dead people huddled around one of the video screens, which is playing some kind of orientation video. I stop in my tracks to watch it, thinking it might give us some useful information about the netherworld.

"Welcome to the First Court of Dìyù, penitents! If you're watching this, you're in Hell!" There are subtitles in Chinese and English, so I can follow along without Kevin having to translate. The video is narrated by a cheery netherworld demon in a black boiler suit. Sitting next to him is a tall white-faced demon with a white boiler suit and an unnaturally long, protruding tongue that hangs out of his mouth, even though he doesn't say anything. Black Boiler Suit continues, "When it's your turn to go before Judge Qínguǎng, he will review all the misdeeds of your most recent life on the Mirror of Retribution."

The screen cuts to footage of a trial. It didn't really click before when Monk and the Guilds were talking about the Ten Courts of Dìyù, but it turns out the First Court is actually a *court*room. Unlike the animal-headed guards or the boiler suit–clad demons narrating the orientation video, whose faces are as black and white as the two halves of a yin-yang symbol, Judge Qínguǎng looks more or less like an ordinary person, except ancient. His wrinkles sag so much, it's like his skin is a size too big for his body. Instead of lawyers, the poor dead person on trial stands in front of a giant circular mirror made out of polished bronze, placed on a pedestal about ten feet off the ground. The dead guy looks into the mirror, but instead of showing his reflection, the mirror shows a montage of scenes as if they're playing on a movie projector. They seem to be scenes throughout his life of varying degrees of badness: stealing his baby sibling's red envelopes, pushing another kid into a lake, parking in an accessible parking spot despite not being a disabled person, calling his mom only to ask for money.

"After reviewing all your negative karma, the Judge will determine what punishments you will have to endure in the subsequent Courts, and for what duration," says Black Boiler Suit. "But until then, just sit back, relax, and please, cry all you want. It only makes us stronger."

A cheesy old-fashioned laugh track follows this, uh, "joke." A cutesy cartoon graphic reading FREQUENTLY ASKED QUESTIONS! pops up on the screen. White Boiler

Suit, whose unnaturally long-fingered white hands are holding a stack of cards, flips one over. Though he doesn't say anything, the subtitles read: *I'm not supposed to be here! This is a mistake!*

Black Boiler Suit says, "That's what they all say! Also, that's not a question. Next!"

White Boiler Suit turns over the next card: *Why are we all dressed the same?* To which Black Boiler Suit delivers the punchline: "It makes it easier for our torturers to not see you as individuals!" to more recorded laughter.

Dr. Fang told me the netherworld is not an amusement park, but that's the vibe I'm getting from this video. The demonic beings who run Dìyù sure seem to be having fun tormenting the dead, at least when they're not extorting them for cash.

"A better place, huh?" I scoff, shaking my head in disgust as I follow the spool out of the First Court.

TEN

Blood Is Thicker than Water and That's Actually Kinda Relevant to the Plot

We continue following the spool through the First Court. As we approach the front of the room, we can see the judge's bench and the Mirror of Retribution.

"Should we get rid of them?" Kevin holds up the Staff, but I remember Ox-Head and Horse-Face taunting us about how calling attention to ourselves could just slow us down. I'm about 95 percent sure that they were just saying that to intimidate us into handing over money. Heck, they're probably still laughing at us for falling for it. But to my frustration, I can't get the 5 percent uncertainty out of my mind.

Sighing, I shake my head. I switch off the flashlight so we aren't emitting a glaring light in the dark room and keep tracking the thread with just the light of the phone screen, tilted down toward the floor. It keeps on rolling until suddenly it rolls smack into the middle of a wall.

For a moment I stare at it, confused. But then I put my hand out, and sure enough, it opens up a hidden door. The spool resumes rolling, and Kevin and I follow after it.

We find ourselves in a long, empty, and very dark corridor. I turn on the phone's flashlight again and look at the spool. My first thought is that it's shown us a secret passageway. But when it leads us to a corner, I look around and glimpse a disoriented-looking woman emerging from another door in the wall, and I realize we're actually in a maze.

When I see the spool rolling straight in the dead woman's direction, my heart starts pounding. But she doesn't pay us any attention as she wanders down the maze, nor do any of the other dead people we cross paths with.

"Why don't they just refuse to move?" I wonder aloud. "I mean, sitting in a creepy maze in the dark isn't great, but it has to be better than wherever they're going." We're not even in the later Courts yet, and just going through the maze is torture already. Our shoes make a crunching sound as we walk, and when I look down, I discover that the paths of the maze are paved with tiny crushed stones. Kevin and I are wearing sneakers, but the dead people are all barefoot, and it wouldn't be long before their feet are in serious pain.

Kevin shrugs. "They're not going to be down here forever, right? Just however long they need to pay off all the bad things they did in their previous life," he says. "So maybe it's, like, they might as well just get the torturing over with."

"I guess that's one way to look at being tortured." But then I see a bedraggled-looking dead man holding his arms out for balance, like Mona Li after she first learned to walk on her own. When I look down toward his bare feet, I see that he's not actually taking steps off the ground, but being pushed by some invisible force toward whatever horrors await him.

I guess that's why we haven't seen any more guards or other netherworld staff around to make sure the dead people don't try to escape. This seems like a good time to try and call Thida, so I pull up the keypad on the phone and call the number on my arm.

It doesn't even ring. No signal.

Ugh. I had doubted whether this thing could even work in the first place, but it's still disappointing that I can't let my best friend and my aunt know we made it inside safely. As I put the useless phone away, my skin crawls. Guess we'll have to try the needle magic when we have the time to embroider a whole message.

It looks like I'm stuck down here with Kevin Chengsson.

"So what can you do?" I say finally. Realizing how insulting that sounds, I add, "My aunt said everyone in the Guilds has to master a particular skill."

Kevin pauses for quite a long time before responding, and I can already tell I'm not going to like his answer. "Oh, yeah. I'm, you know, still working on that."

Bicycle on a wire. Bicycle on a wire.

"Well, you keep doing that," I say, feeling even more awkward than when this conversation started. I've never really been good at talking to people I don't already know. I always thought that was one of the few things I get from my mom. Most people don't realize it because my mom is so confident and makes jokes at parties, but she doesn't really hang out with anyone aside from us and Auntie Kathie . . . or at least, that's what we all thought.

Are all her friends in the Weavers or the other Guilds? Is that why I've never met a single friend of hers? Before I wondered if she felt guilty at all about keeping this entire part of her life from us, because I just couldn't believe she could do that. But now I also wonder: Didn't it feel *lonely*?

"Did your aunt tell you about the red thread of fate?" It takes me a moment to remember that that was the deal Kevin made with my aunt in exchange for coming down here with me. Even though he doesn't sound like he's judging, I still feel embarrassed to shake my head. I get that my mom made a promise, but it still stings that this random kid who isn't even in the Weavers knows this stuff about my own family when I didn't know any of it.

Kevin explains, "The red thread of fate is an invisible string tied around the ankles of people who are destined to be each other's true love. Your Auntie Kathie's special skill is finding it."

"Really?" It must be like the Spindle of Fate where you can't do it on yourself, because that ability obviously hasn't done my aunt's own love life any good. Not that I'd tell Kevin that, though. Mom is big on family loyalty: She complains all the time about Auntie Kathie's terrible taste in boyfriends, but she goes nuclear if anyone else tries to judge her little sister.

Against my will, I flash back to the last conversation I had with my own younger sister. It makes me feel a little better to remember that Mom could rant about Auntie Kathie's choices, but my aunt couldn't possibly doubt how much she loved her. But is that just something I'm telling myself to feel better, like the useless things that adults told me so I wouldn't be sad? Or something even worse—an excuse?

"Yeah!" Kevin says. I'm startled before I remember the conversation we were having before my mind started going down dark places. "So she can tell me who my soulmate is."

Somehow, my opinion of the Guilds sinks even lower. All these mystical nerds devoting their lives to studying literal magic, and the only one brave enough to come with me was some romantic goober looking for his waifu.

As we continue following the unwinding spool through the maze, I notice a sickening, slightly metallic smell in the air. The stench gets stronger as we follow the line of red, and I realize it's not my imagination.

"Uh . . . is that blood?" The gruesome images on Wood Elder's painting of Dìyù flash through my mind. There must be a *lot* of it for the smell to be this strong. What kind of unspeakable tortures are we heading toward?

Holding my breath, I march forward down the hallway and into the Second Court. But suddenly the ground disappears under my feet, and when I look down, I realize I've walked right off a diving board. I scream as I plummet straight into the middle of an immense pool of blood.

The stench is awful. On instinct, I hold my breath, but quickly realize that's not an option when I'm half-submerged in liquid. The pool is also filled with countless bodies of dead people, struggling to swim across the blood. Some of them aren't moving, like they're *dead* dead, but then they twitch and start flailing around, as if coming back to "life." But if I were to pass out here, I could drown . . . and it won't be *anything* like falling asleep.

I flash back to my recurring nightmare over the past ten days, the one that weighed down on me like a five-hundred-pound monster sitting on my chest each night while I lay in bed. Mom struggling for air. Mom thrashing around desperately in the water. Even though I know now that she didn't really drown, that doesn't make it any less terrifying.

My throat suddenly becomes tight, and my limbs twitch all over. "Kevin?" I call out. I instinctively had shut my eyes, but when I open them again to look for him, I discover that the mass of flailing bodies in the slow-moving current had separated us, and I can't see him anywhere. "Kevin!"

I start to panic, but then I hear him responding, "What is it?" When I turn my head, I see him swimming toward me.

"Can—" It's hard to get the words out. My stomach lurches, but then I feel a hand on my arm.

"Don't take this the wrong way," Kevin says, "but you don't look okay."

"I'm okay. It's just that I feel like I'm going to die." I guess when I put it like that, it's no different from how I've been feeling for the past ten days. We grab on to the Staff of Mùlián like it's a pool noodle, holding it like a bar in front of us and dog-paddling.

"Oh, shoot. Can you not swim?"

"I could," I say weakly. "My mom's car was found in the ocean, so we thought she'd drowned."

"Oh, *shoot*," Kevin mutters. I look at my hand. The spool is still tied to my finger, but it's just floating in the blood, unable to show us a way out.

Taking short but steady breaths, I look out at the teeming mass of flailing bodies and limbs all around us. As I lift my head above the blood, I notice there's a lifeguard chair on a platform about fifty feet above our heads, next to the extension of maze that becomes a diving board. At first I think a demon is sitting in the chair, but then I realize it's just a statue. I roll my eyes in disgust. Dìyù obviously put that there just to rub it in the dead people's faces that they're drowning. My irritation at such a stupid, mean joke gives me a surgc of motivation.

"Mom wasn't in the First Court, so she must have ended up here or made it out somehow. But the spool won't roll in the blood, so it can't show us either way." Talking out loud clears my head a little, so I keep doing it. "The spool can't roll in the liquid, unless . . . I put it on something flat?" I tug on the thread to pull the spool in, like I'm reeling in a fish, and place it on the Staff. But as soon as it starts rolling, it falls right back into the blood.

"The Staff of Mùlián is too thin. What else do

I have?" I take the phone out of my pocket, hoping the blood doesn't ruin what limited use it already had. Kevin takes it and I set the spool on it. It rolls in a straight line across and then just falls off back toward the blood. It's too short to tell if it might have become tangled.

"The phone is too short." Dismayed, I put it back into the purse and look around. But all I see are bodies, flailing and thrashing and drowning . . .

"Oh! I got it!" Kevin says. "Roll it on me!" He planks over in the blood with what I have to admit is an admirable lack of concern about getting his face all bloody.

I put the spool on his back. I hold my breath as it starts to roll again, only to roll straight off him. I try again, setting it on the base of Kevin's neck so it has his entire height to roll, but it just makes an angle and rolls straight into the blood again.

The thread didn't become *tangled*, which is what Auntie Kathie said it would do if the Spindle of Fate was near. If Mom isn't here, then we have to get out of the Second Court. But the "pool" is big enough that I can't see the end of it. With all the people in the blood, it could take hours to swim across.

I look at the thread tied to my finger, the spool submerged in the blood. Suddenly, it hits me where it's pointing.

My throat feels tight again, and my head becomes so faint, my vision starts to blur dark red. A small voice inside my head protests that I don't even know if this will work, but I tell it to shut up. I have to try.

"I think it's trying to point *down*. I'm going to—I'm going to try and see what's below us." Remembering that clothes weigh you down, I take off Kevin's jacket. Even though I might regret it *again*, I mentally run through the rest of what I learned the sleepless night after I used Thida's phone to look up *is drowning peaceful?* My stomach lurching, I add, "Hey, Kevin? If I don't come up, don't go in after me—"

"What?" Kevin blurts out. "What are you talking about?" For the first time, his voice rises in frustration. "Look, I know you didn't want me to be here, and I get it, but I'm not going to just sit here and do nothing if you start drowning—"

"No, that's exactly the problem! When people start to drown, they usually p-panic and try to grab whatever's around. Sometimes that's people who try to rescue them. A lot of people die when they try to save someone else from drowning and get pulled down instead."

Kevin's eyes widen. "Oh. Oh, *shoot*."

"Yeah. I looked it up." You could say it's a *violent* way to die: You can literally kill someone else by mistake.

Kevin gulps. "So how are you supposed to save someone from drowning, then?"

"Instead of trying to pull them out of the water yourself, you're supposed to hand or throw them something to grab on to. That's why lifeguards carry those floatation thingies."

"Oh, I get it. So if you don't come up, I'll push the Staff down so you can grab on to it."

"Yeah." Even though my nostrils could kill me for it, I take a deep, deep breath. Then I let go of the Staff and dive straight down.

Blood instantly rushes into my nose, and I have to tamp down the overwhelming urge to gag. But I puff up my cheeks and keep diving downward.

It's hard to see anything at all through the haze—all I can make out is red liquid and kicking legs. But I keep diving, my arms stretched outward, and it's not long before I feel it—a hard surface. While the blood pool looked to be endlessly long and wide, it can't be much more than six feet deep, like an average swimming pool. After all, why would it be? That's more than deep enough for people to drown in.

I flash back to what Dr. Hsu said about the Staff of Mùlián: It can smash through the walls of Dìyù. Can it smash through the floors, too? That seems logical, but there's no way of knowing where we'll fall into on the other side—it could be a random closet or right into a volcano.

But then I feel a thread, and I realize the spool is rolling toward the bottom with me as I dive down. I might not have a lot of faith in the Guilds, but surely my mom's spool wouldn't point me in this direction if it was more dangerous than just swimming across the blood.

I glide forward in the blood, then swim back up. "I think I know how we can get out," I say as I come up for air. I have to take a moment to wipe the blood out of my eyes before continuing (though what I really want is to wipe it out of my mouth, too, because it tastes like salt and metal and it's disgusting).

But after I do, I see an alarming sight. Multiple dead people have also grabbed on to the Staff of Mùlián for support, and even more dead people have grabbed on to *those* dead people. They're focusing all their energy on keeping their heads above the blood, making no attempt to swim or climb to safety. Their combined, panicked strength is enough to nearly pull the Staff out of Kevin's arms.

"I thought it was okay to let the first guy grab the Staff so he wouldn't drown, but then a bunch of other people got the same idea," Kevin explains sheepishly. Kevin has wrapped his arms around the Staff and is holding on tight, but there are way more of them than there are of us.

"Well, we need to get them off! I think the Staff is our way out. I found a surface to smash through at the bottom of the pool. Let's go!"

I try to yank the Staff out of the dead people's hands, but it's like playing tug-of-war against a building. Kevin reaches out to help me, but that barely produces a budge. Fear crawls up my throat. Not only are we outnumbered, we're outnumbered by people who are drowning, who are literally holding on to the Staff for dear life, or whatever it is they have down here.

"What are we going to do?" I try not to fully panic; that's how people drown. "We need to bring the Staff to the bottom."

Suddenly, I get an idea. "If we can't pull the Staff down, we can *weigh* it down so it sinks to the bottom."

I scoop up the spool, using the thread to tie the

purse with the phone inside to the Staff. Kevin reaches around the dead people to pull on the metal topper with the rings on the head of Mùlián's Staff. To my surprise, it comes off with a few twists, and Kevin adds it to the bag, too. He also unzips his jacket and adds the painting of Auntie Kathie's house before zipping the bag shut.

Kevin shoots me a look. "So then we go after it?"

I had figured we could dive down after the sinking Staff and then simply push it against the bottom of the pool. But then to my horror I realize that isn't going to work.

"It's really hard to see inside the blood. What if we can't find it again once we're down there?"

Kevin replies, "We could tie ourselves to the Staff." My own blood runs cold as I realize what that means. But Kevin just pulls out the strings of his hoodie and ties his wrist then mine to the Staff.

I imagine what it'd be like not just to dive into the blood, but to sink. Kicking and thrashing in the blood. What if we panic and can't untie ourselves again?

But what are my other options? With the dead people holding on to the Staff, it could take forever to swim across. And we have no chance making it through the rest of Dìyù without the Staff.

“Take a deep breath,” I say. “Whatever you do, don’t panic.”

Kevin and I take the deepest breaths we can. Then I drop the bag full of metal into the blood. It sinks, along with the Staff of Mùlián. The Staff slips out of the arms of the dead people. A spark of hope hits me as I watch it go.

But then it’s covered in hands again. Frantic people cling to it even as it no longer floats, dragging them—and us—down with it.

I squeeze tighter on to the Staff as we sink. I feel a hand there, and at first I think Kevin had the same idea, but then I realize I can’t be sure with all the dead people. My eardrums feel like they’re on fire as we sink to the bottom of the pool, into the deep red. Everything is red and dark, and I feel the panic coming on.

But just as instinctively, my other hand leaps to the red string around my neck. Suddenly, as if by magic, all panic leaves my body. I trace the elaborate knots, remembering what I have to do and who I have to find.

When my entire body is submerged, I push down on Mùlián’s Staff. There’s a tremendous *CRACK!* and all I want to do is cover my hurting ears as we burst through the Second Court.

ELEVEN

CRUEL AND UNUSUAL NOURISHMENT

Well, technically we fall through. Because with the giant hole that we just created at the bottom of the pool, it's more like we tumble down a waterfall of blood. Since Kevin and I were tied to the Staff, we slam against each other. It hurts, but also breaks each other's fall as we hit the floor.

"Oh shoot, we made it!" Kevin says, gasping for air. He bursts into laughter, nervously at first, but then with genuine relief and delight at being alive. I rub my ears, which are still sore from sinking to the bottom of the pool, and try my best to wipe the blood out of my eyes and hair. Kevin and I are both drenched with gore, including the insides of my nostrils. It's super gross, but also kinda cool that we look like the characters still standing at the end of an action movie.

"We did," I manage to say, also gasping. We lie there on the ground for a moment, taking loud, wonderful breaths. This really isn't a nice place—like the rest of Dìyù, it's cold and dark and if I listen closely, I'm pretty sure I can hear screaming in the distance. But it's dry and full of air. Right now, I love it.

"I panicked," Kevin admits. It takes a moment for me to realize what he means, as the last thing I said to him before we went under comes back to me. "I'm glad you didn't."

I flash back to everything I read about drowning panic. Kevin is smiling from ear to ear, basking in the bliss of not drowning, but he must have been truly terrified. For a moment, I wonder at how I didn't panic, too. But then my hand instinctively leaps to the red string pendant around my blood-red throat again, and I recall how my own fear instantly vanished as I ran my fingers over the knots and loops, giving me the clarity of mind to push the Staff against the bottom of the pool. In the moment it had felt like magic, but maybe that's because it was—specifically, my mom's protective magic.

Kevin uses his free hand to untie the hoodie string binding us to the Staff, while I untie the spool around the handbag and unzip it to check on our magical items. The cheap leather soaked up the blood red like a sponge, and I smile thinking about my mom telling Auntie Lilli how to identify real designer handbags versus cheap imitations—looks like the joss paper handbag is really a joss paper knockoff. But the blood has already clotted, and since the bag was zipped shut, the inside isn't even damp. I'm relieved to see the painting of Auntie Kathie's apartment intact, since that's our way home.

The phone is another story. It must have been damaged by the brief time I placed it in the blood to try and make the spool roll on it, because it won't turn on when I try to unlock it. We're probably not going to get reception down here anyway so it's not like it's the biggest loss, but still.

Kevin takes the metal topper with rings and screws it back onto the Staff of Mùlián. Meanwhile, I address the spool, its thread miraculously straight and untangled despite sinking into the blood and plummeting when we crashed through the floor. "Take me to Mom."

The spool takes off, and we follow it back through the maze. It's much creepier without the light of the phone. Kevin takes out his laser pointer again and points it straight at the ground, which is enough to allow us to follow the thread, but it's still nerve-racking to be fumbling around in the dark. Also, with our sense of vision impaired, the echoes of dead people screaming in the distance suddenly become a *lot* more noticeable, which makes it even worse. Now I can also hear a gushing sound like the wind blowing, pushing the dead people toward whatever punishments they'd each earned in life.

"So what's your mom like?" Kevin says. He tries to sound nonchalant, but he talks a little quicker than usual, and I think he's nervous about wandering through the netherworld in the dark, too.

"Oh. Uh." I'm surprised at how hard it is all of a sudden to talk about her. This should be the literal easiest subject to talk about since it's the only thing I have been able to think about every minute of every day since she went missing. I'm not sure if I can technically say the grief is still raw if she never actually died, but I guess that doesn't just make all the pain from the past ten days go away. "I thought you knew her already?"

"Yeah, but not as a mom," Kevin replies. "And I only see her when all the Guilds get together, which is only, like, a couple of times a year."

"Well. She was—*is* a really talented seamstress.

We own a tailor shop, so she made all of our clothes when I was growing up."

I must be blowing Kevin's mind right now with all of these shocking revelations. Who would have thought the head of the Weavers was good at working with cloth?

I squeeze the red string around my neck as I rattle off details about my mom. "My mom *is* super hard-working, a perfectionist, and a neat freak. She's legit really good at what she does, though. Like, I've seen her tell some of our regular customers to just throw their clothes away instead of asking her to fix it because it's ugly, and they still keep coming back because they're so happy with her work."

I feel like I'm reading off a list. Everything I've just said is true, and it's a pretty good summary of my mom. But he could have gotten all of that from any of the other Weavers, or even our regular customers. On the other hand, would it feel any less inadequate to tell him about my mom's coin flip trick, or that her favorite book is *Crying in H Mart*, or that she lost both her parents in her senior year of college, so she had to drop out to become a parent to my teenage aunt?

Because what I'm not telling Kevin is that my mom is uptight, judgmental, and really annoying. Sometimes she drove me so crazy that I started imagining Auntie Kathie was my mom instead so I could live in Las Vegas or sail around the world with her instead of having to help out at the tailor shop. My first attempt at a screenplay when I was in fifth grade was basically a self-insert fanfic if that was actually my life, but my tattletale little sister found it and showed my parents without realizing what I'd written. I thought Mom would get mad at me, but after she didn't say anything for two days, I freaked out and confronted my dad about it. He tried to act like everything was okay, but he sucks at pretending—he thinks he doesn't, but it's *really* obvious—and finally he caved and admitted that it made her cry. I told her that I didn't mean any of it and I was just blowing off steam. But that wasn't true. I used to imagine it all the time whenever we had an argument.

That's what I felt about her. It's not how I felt about her all the time, and it isn't *all* I felt about her. Not even close. But it's what I would have told Kevin if he had asked me this question more than ten days ago, because I didn't keep it inside. Thida knows because I complained to her constantly, and so does my sister, and my dad, and worst of all, so does my mom, because one time I told her to her face. But I can't tell Kevin that.

Fluorescent lighting appears up ahead as the spool leads us into a different kind of court: a food court. Not like the food courts in malls or airports with different vendors, but like the cafeteria-style "food court" Chinese restaurant near our local H Mart. There's a counter along one wall where dead people are lined up for food, and long metal tables like in a prison cafeteria. Some of the people are drenched in blood, like us, but others are dry. Based on the menu items displayed over the counter and what I can see on the tables, the only food option appears to be plain rice.

"So I'm guessing the food is really bad here?" Kevin says. "Is that why ghosts are always hungry?"

But then I hear a *clink!* of metal. I turn my head toward the sound and see an unfortunate dead woman spitting out her rice—or at least, it was rice. When she gags into her bowl, shiny metal pellets tumble out instead.

The dead man sitting across from her flings his own bowl away in disgust. But others around the tables barely even react. I'm startled to notice then that many of the people in the Third Court are very thin, some little more than skeletons. How long have they been here?

Shuddering, I quietly thank Dr. Fang for her grain of rice. But then, as I watch the spool continue to roll without tangling, my stomach churns.

"My mom has been here for ten days. Can she survive this long without food or water?" My voice comes out a whisper, like it's too horrible to say aloud.

For a moment, Kevin furrows his brow, not saying anything. I don't want to panic in Dìyù. Panic gets you killed. My throat starts to tighten. One horrible thought leads to another, and I wonder, what if we follow the spool through Dìyù just to find my mom dead of thirst . . .

But then Kevin's eyes light up. "Oh, I know! She could survive on the blood from the Second Court."

To give credit where it's due, that does snap me out of the panic that had threatened to overwhelm me, only to make me feel differently sick to my stomach. "Um, eww?"

"I'm serious! Have you ever had pork blood? If you let it just sit out in a container or something, it becomes solid after a while. It feels kind of like tofu! My grandma used to eat it with her congee."

Āh Mā also makes porridge for breakfast, but I've never seen pork blood like he's talking about. Mom probably has, though. To my surprise given how he started with this, I actually feel a lot better knowing there's a way my mom could find food down here. But before I can thank him, Kevin turns and walks toward the bowl of "rice" that the one guy had tossed onto the floor.

"What are you doing?" I call after him, stunned. "Did you not see what happened to that lady's food just now?"

"The rice is barely cooked!" He scoops all the rice back into the bowl and returns to me. Indeed, the grains are so undercooked they make a rattling sound as he runs. "You can put the phone in it and it'll draw out the blood. I tried it after I dropped my phone in the toilet."

I skip the first question that comes to my mind and go right to the second. "And that actually worked?"

"Sort of. It turned back on again, but it still died a week later. But we shouldn't be here that long, right?"

I watch skeptically as Kevin takes the phone and

submerges it into the bowl of rice. Even though the blood had mostly clotted by now, the rice does seem to absorb liquid inside the hardware, the white grains growing moist and red. After a while, he hands the phone back to me.

When I press the power button, the lock screen appears.

"You're a genius," I say in disbelief. I switch on the flashlight because it is still pretty dark in here and it's creepy. But to my disappointment, Thida still hasn't returned my call or texted me.

Auntie Kathie had figured that we might not get reception, so hopefully they won't be too worried if they don't hear from me—or at least, not much more worried than they already are about my being in Dìyù. Thida always rolls her eyes about her mom insisting she text her whenever she arrives at my apartment even though she lives less than ten minutes away from me by skateboard. But I can kinda understand now; I'm still disappointed that I can't do the same.

But then I realize that I can. I unbutton my shorts pocket and take out the handkerchief that Auntie Kathie had given me.

"Hey, did you hear from your aunt?" Kevin asks.

"Oh, no," I say, crestfallen. "I was just thinking I could try to send a message to her, too, since my mom taught me to sew. But I realized I don't have a needle."

"Do you have a hair pin or something?" Kevin gestures at my braid. As it turns out, I do. I pluck it out of my sticky hair and carefully tie one end of the string around it, then poke the end of the hairpin through the handkerchief. The tip of the pin is bigger and duller than a sewing needle, so it's clunky to poke holes through the cloth, and they're also bigger than regular stitches. My letters arc childlike and disproportionate like a kindergartner's handwriting, but it works.

I manage to stitch: *we r here*, using *r* instead of *are*, like my boomer relatives when they text, since it takes me a long time to sew each of the letters. I'm not as good at it as my sister, but I'm actually not bad, which I'm pretty sure frustrated Mom more. But I'm out of practice, and it's really awkward with the makeshift needle on top of that. It won't be very practical for me to message Auntie Kathie and Thida with this method while we're making our way through Dìyù. But hopefully they can get this and know we haven't gotten ourselves killed already.

Just as I finish stitching the last *e*, however, someone shouts, "Hey! You aren't penitents!" I spin around to see a demonic cafeteria worker has emerged from behind the counter, shaking his fist and metal serving ladle at us. He looks more or less like a large, angry human man except for his bright green skin. He sports a red boiler suit the color of cooked lobster, and he isn't wearing a hairnet or any other kind of head covering despite his thick, flowing hair and sideburns, because Dìyù obviously isn't concerned about hygiene when the people in this food court are (1) already dead and (2) supposed to be miserable.

With alarming agility, the demon puts one meaty arm on the glass sneeze guards over the rice, then catapults himself over the counter at us, like a professional wrestler plunging off the ropes. Heart pounding, I reach for the Staff of Mùlián, but Kevin beats me to it. He rings the Staff, producing a thundering *CLANG!* The food court demon loses his balance mid-lunge and face-plants right into the hard tile floor.

I look down at the demon, curled up into a ball and writhing at my feet. "Are you kidding me? *This* is what this thing would have done to Ox-Head and Horse-Face?"

When he gets up, Kevin rings the Staff again, and the demon immediately runs in the other direction. The dead people, who had been unfazed by the ringing, burst into applause and jeer after him as he runs away.

"Wow, that was easy," Kevin says, looking at the Staff with admiration. But as I watch the demon flee, I suddenly feel confused.

"That guy could tell we're not supposed to be here because we're not dressed like everyone else. Shouldn't my mom have been spotted by now, too?" And why wouldn't she want to be? Unlike us, she doesn't *want* to be in Dìyù, not even a little bit. She just needed to get away from Monk. And if one of the demons working in Dìyù spotted Mom and reported her to upper management, why would she still be here?

Kevin's sleepy-looking eyes widen as he picks up what I'm putting down. "Didn't Water Elder say it takes a really long time to get anything done down here? Maybe they put her in a waiting room somewhere and she's still there."

That's honestly a much nicer thought than her running around somewhere in the torture-labyrinth part of Dìyù. "One thing's for sure: We're not going to get any help from asking the staff." My disgust at the corrupt netherworld guards rises again in my chest like acid reflux. They'd probably just try to extort more money out of us.

But it's not worth getting mad about again, not when Mom is waiting for me. I return my attention to the spool. While we were focused on the demon worker, the spool had magically rolled up and over the food court counter. We climb onto the counter and follow the unwinding thread as it rolls under the door of a staff restroom. Kevin taps the door with the end of the Staff, and it immediately falls clean off its hinges and onto the tile floor.

I look around the empty restroom, confused. It's one of those bathrooms with just a single toilet, which is stuffed with pamphlets that Dìyù staff must have unsuccessfully tried to flush, causing water to overflow onto the floor. The pamphlets all show a woman sporting a spotless white pantsuit and a snazzy undercut, crossing her arms. They're written in English as well as Chinese, so I can read the text on the cover: NEED COMPASSION? CALL ON GUĀNYĪN, GODDESS OF MERCY! That's nice, though I have to wonder if the wait must be pretty long. I would think that mercy is in hot demand in Hell.

"Why would the spool lead us here?" I wonder aloud. I look down at our feet and then I notice it: a tangle in the thread. At first it's just a single knot, but as the spool keeps rolling around the empty room, the thread becomes more and more tangled.

TWELVE

THE FOURTH COURT (THE REAL ONE)

For a moment, I'm afraid to even believe it. My heart is pounding so hard it actually hurts.

Mom is near.

I look at the spool, now stuck in a hopeless mass of thread. I was so desperate for the spool to start tangling that I didn't really worry about what it would mean when it did. I now know for sure that Mom is close, but thanks to her pendant's anti-tracking feature, we'll have to find her totally on our own, with no more magic Weaver Google Maps to point us the way.

"What is it?" Kevin asks.

"The spool tangles when . . ." My breath hitches. "When my mom's nearby."

His sleepy-looking eyes pop wide open.

Kevin looks around the tiny bathroom. "Did it lead

us in here just to throw us off? Or was it going to show us another shortcut?" He picks up the Staff of Mùlián and moves toward the wall.

"Hey, don't do that while we're inside! Not unless you wanna bring down the ceiling on top of us."

I exit the bathroom, untying the thread around my finger and stuffing the mass of tangled thread inside the handbag as I do. I look around the back room of the food court and spot an elevator in the adjacent wall. I guess that's how the Dìyù staff move around without having to go through the confusing maze.

"The thread didn't tangle until we climbed over the counter. What if it's because Mom is in the next Court?"

But before I can move for the elevator, I spot the cafeteria worker in the shiny red boiler suit, pointing at us from across the room. Running alongside him is a freakishly tall and thin demon in a white boiler suit who I recognize as one of the creeps from the orientation video in the First Court. He had looked tall on camera next to his pint-sized, black-suited counterpart, but in person he has to be nearly seven feet tall, towering over even the large cafeteria worker demon.

"He came back? Seriously?" Kevin rings the Staff of Mùlián again. Red Boiler Suit has already vanished, but White Boiler Suit keeps running, seemingly unfazed.

Kevin looks at the Staff, dumbfounded. "Why isn't this working?" He rings it again, but again, the white-suited demon keeps running toward us without batting an eye. He's close enough that I can see his hideous demonic face now, his long tongue flapping out the side of his open mouth like a dog sticking its head out the car window.

I remember him silently holding up the *Frequently Asked Questions* cue cards in the orientation video without reading them aloud.

Suddenly, I know why the Staff doesn't seem to affect him. "He's deaf! Run!"

Thinking fast, Kevin reaches forward and grabs the bowl of rice we'd used to resurrect the phone, which he'd left on the counter when we'd climbed over. He flings the ceramic bowl at the silent netherworld demon, who instinctively covers his ghastly white face with his freakishly long fingers while we bolt for the elevator. I push the down button, frantically tugging at my red string pendant as we wait for the elevator doors to open. Once they do, I pull Kevin inside and slam the button to close them.

But as I look for the fourth-floor button, I frown.

There are ten buttons, running straight down the wall in a line, and every single one of them reads *4*.

"Uh, which one do I press?"

Kevin looks at the buttons. "Some Chinese elevators skip the fourth floor because the number four is considered unlucky. It's because it sounds just like the word for *death*. So I guess in the netherworld, *every* floor is the fourth floor?"

Oh, I've heard about that. Mom roasts Dad a lot for his obsession with puns, but it's probably the most Chinese thing about him. Now it's just unnecessarily annoying. Sighing, I reach for the fourth *4* from the bottom before remembering that the Courts go down. So I press the fourth *4* from the top instead, and sure enough, the elevator goes down a single floor before the doors open.

We step out into the Fourth Court (or the Fourth Fourth Court).

It's . . . empty. Weirdly empty. After shoving through the masses of suffering bodies in the first three Courts, it's kind of a relief but also unsettling. The phone light reveals long hallways of numbered doors.

Kevin glances over his shoulder toward the elevator. "Should we get moving? What if he comes looking for us?"

The silent demon didn't see us getting into the elevator, but if he looks behind the counter and finds we've vanished, it shouldn't be too hard for him to figure out where we went. Would he try to look for us himself or is he on his way to report us to King Yama?

I look uneasily at the doors, dreading what kind of horrors are behind each. I move toward the nearest door, but then run across the hall to one a bit farther down. I throw the door open and slam it shut as soon as Kevin's inside, not bothering to be quiet since the demon wouldn't hear it if he came after us.

I brace myself to find ourselves in some kind of horrific torture chamber. But inside is just a single penitent, a dead woman sitting cross-legged on a bed in front of a projector screen that takes up the entire back wall. At the sound of the door slamming shut, the woman had turned around to gawk at us. Not everyone that we've seen in Dìyù has been old, but I'm startled—and sad—to see she's really young to be dead, not even Auntie Kathie's age.

"Nǐ shì shéi?" she asks. That much I can understand—*who are you?*—but I let Kevin do the talking. While they do, I glance around. It's better lit here with the giant video screen—which actually kind of hurts my eyes after growing semi-used to the dark—so I can see there's not much here besides a bed and a screen that shows an elderly man in a nursing home, screaming in pain.

I watch Kevin's face as he speaks with the woman. He has to shout to be heard over the video. After a few seconds of getting nowhere, the woman finally picks up a remote and pauses the screen. Kevin doesn't try to hide his reactions, so even only understanding every other word, I can see the horror in his eyes as he takes in what she's telling him. It's enough to wish we could've stayed at the part where Kevin couldn't hear her over the video. But when he turns to me, he looks more relaxed.

"This is the Court of the Wrongful Dead. It's for people who were murdered or who died because they were wronged in some way," he explains. "So normally after you go through all the Courts, you're reincarnated into your next life, right? But people who carry a strong grudge with them are at risk of not crossing over and becoming vengeful ghosts. So the people who are sent down here get to watch the suffering of the people who wronged them until they hopefully release their grudge." Kevin's eyes dart toward the woman as he whispers, "She's watching the guy who killed her die."

That makes me feel a little better about what's on the screen behind us, but I kind of wonder if this would really make *her* feel better. She's so young, and while her killer's death is hard to watch, he at least seems to have gotten to live to an old age. That doesn't seem fair at all to me. But what else is new here?

"Did your aunt tell you how close your mom would have to be to throw off the spool?" Kevin asks.

"No." My stomach sinks as I realize what this means. Mom could be in the Fifth Court, or the Sixth Court, or even lower than that. And come to think of it, does *close* mean in terms of distance or time? If it was the elevator nearby that caused the spool to start spiraling off course, she could be all the way in the Ninth or Tenth Court, since finding the elevator meant we could go there within a matter of seconds.

The spool can't help us anymore, and now the Staff is also useless against the white-suited demon. If he hadn't seen us, we could try and search every twist and turn of the remaining Courts. But that's more than half of Dìyù, and what if White Boiler Suit comes after us? There has to be a faster way.

"Hey, weren't you saying your mom should have been seen by the demons?" Kevin says after I've been silent for a while. "Maybe we should try and figure out where she would have been taken after that?"

Oh! Right! I'd totally forgotten about that. "So . . . we'd be going *toward* the demons?" That seems like a bold move, and potentially risky now that we know there's at least one demon that the Staff of Mùlián doesn't work against. But it's a lead.

"Okay. Let's do it."

I push open the door a crack and stick out the phone, illuminating the empty halls. "It looks clear." Tentatively I step out of the room; Kevin thanks the dead woman before joining me.

"It's quiet here without all the screaming," he remarks as we walk back toward the elevator.

I hadn't even noticed that I'd gotten used to the screams of the penitents in the background. As relieved as I am that they're gone, that kind of makes me uncomfortable. "Do you feel bad for them?" he asks. "The people in Dìyù."

I had kind of tried to avoid looking at them, to be honest. "Yeah," I admit. "Do you?"

"Yeah," Kevin says. "I guess my mom would say they deserve it. And I'm sure some of them were, like, murderers and racists and stuff. But I don't know. I'm glad that they won't be here forever."

"Yeah, I know what you mean." I don't really have a problem with bad people getting punished for their actions. I know if it were up to me, I would gleefully send whoever hired Monk to kidnap my mom through every single torture that Dìyù has to offer. But seeing all the bodies drowning again and again in the pool of blood, and starving in the Third Court, it was hard not to shudder.

Kevin cranes his neck over his shoulder at the doors, which extend as far as I can see. "There are a lot of doors here," he says. "I guess my dad must have spent time in this Court after he died."

As anxious as I am to find Mom, I can't just not respond to that. At least in my experience, the only thing more awkward than people talking about death is people *not* talking about death.

"Do you miss your dad?"

Kevin shrugs. "I don't really remember him at all. I was three when he died. But I almost feel like I know more about him than about my mom because she talks about him all the time."

So not only does he barely see his mom because she's preoccupied with getting revenge on the people who killed his dad, but when she does see her son, she's just talking constantly about her dead husband? As much as I want to be all *you go, girl, get that revenge*, that does not seem healthy. Suddenly I flash back to the look on my dad's face when he said he felt like he and Mom were fated to meet, and he doesn't even believe in fate. If Mom were really gone, could Dad become so overwhelmed by his own grief that he'd completely forget about Mona Li and me like that?

We arrive back at the elevator. I press the button for the next Court. "What do you know about him?"

"He was a stunt double in Hollywood, like my mom. That's how they met."

"Like, they do the fight scenes in movies? That's so cool."

"Yeah. They were working on the same movie doing the stunts for the lead actors, and then they got together. Isn't that cute?"

I have to admit that is really cute, but it's also super depressing, considering his dad ended up getting murdered by assassins. I had kind of assumed that Kevin wanted to know his soulmate because he watched too many Korean dramas or something, but considering his parents' tragic love story, it's differently sad.

"What movie was that?"

"*Dead Reckoning 3: Dig 200 Graves,*" he replies, and my jaw drops. "It's from this old series about a hitman who has to do one last job before he can retire, but then the zombie apocalypse starts and suddenly he has to fight off all the zombies of everyone he's ever killed—"

"Yeah, I know! I've seen all the *Dead Reckoning* movies! Wait, so does that mean your mom did the fight at the end of *Dead Reckoning 3*, after his girlfriend turns into a zombie and he has to fight her?" When Kevin nods, I almost lose it. "Are you kidding me? That's a *classic*! I mean, the movie was kinda trash, but that's one of the best fights in the whole series! When I watched it, I literally said, *I need to have a scene like that in my movie . . .*"

My voice trails off. I was so caught up fangirling, I didn't realize I had almost revealed the first step in my two-step plan.

"Oh, so you're writing a movie?" Kevin says. "That's so cool! What's it about?"

"Oh. Yeah." I feel a little nervous talking about this, but then again, this kid told me within minutes after we met that his mom has killed nearly a dozen people. He doesn't seem like the type to judge. "I'm trying to write a screenplay for an action movie called *Iron Lotus*. It's about this woman who has bound feet—that was this messed-up thing they used to do to girls' feet, so they'd stay small—"

"Oh yeah, that's what happened to Dr. Fang. That's why she uses a cane."

I frown, thinking he must be wildly mistaken. I did a lot of research into this—Mom says I don't try hard enough to learn something if it's too difficult, but I actually really do when it's something I'm interested in. I just don't see the point in putting a ton of effort into stuff that I don't care about. But anyway, that's how I know foot binding was banned a long time ago. There are still a few really old women who had their feet bound after it was outlawed, but Dr. Fang is way too young for that. I'll have to ask her about that sometime.

"Yeah, so in my movie," I continue, "the girl has bound feet, but she's an amazing martial artist. So she's still really good at fighting with just, like, her hands."

"Oh, dude, that sounds like an awesome movie!" says Kevin. He sounds really sincere, and maybe it's dumb to care too much about it since that's kind of just how he is about everything. But it still feels good. He's the first person to say that. Thida's response when I told her was, "Wait, so how does she move?" I'm still figuring out the details.

Suddenly, I feel like a huge jerk. All this time I've been complaining about my mom being judgmental, and I haven't been any better.

"Hey, Kevin?" I say as the elevator doors open in the Fifth Court. "I'm glad you're here."

THIRTEEN
BOSS BATTLE

Instead of another dark maze, the Fifth Court looks like someone took a corporate campus for a big company, like Apple or Google, and plunked it underground. It's a sprawling hub of interconnected office buildings, densely packed together and surrounded by a circular wall.

Kevin comes to the same conclusion as I do. "Is this where the workers are?"

I walk toward the nearest cluster of buildings. It's almost nice here, or at least not actively hostile to the senses or a creepy void like all the other Courts we've seen. The lighting is better, and the pathways are lined with fake trees and grass, probably because real plants would die without sunlight. The ceiling is painted to look like a blue sky, giving the illusion of being outdoors on a sunny day. I thought the effect was cool when I saw it walking through one of the hotels in Las Vegas, but it feels kind of depressing in a workplace if this really is Dìyù headquarters.

Kevin glances toward a sign peeking out from behind a fake bush. "This is the Department of Records! If your mom turned up somewhere, they might know about it."

From what I've seen of the Dìyù staff so far, I don't want to hold my breath on them being very helpful. But it's the best lead we have. "One way to find out."

I reach for the door handle, only to find it locked. It has one of those scanner pads to check for authorized IDs. But Kevin just pushes the Staff of Mùlián against it, and, to my surprise, it totally works like a key. We continue inside.

This workroom seems to be an open office space, with long tables and low walls dividing different workstations. My first instinct is to saunter in and start wagging the Staff at people, but after that backfired in the Third Court, I decide to try to take a more low-key approach. I duck my head and try to stay to the walls, but no one even notices us. A lot of the workers are wearing headphones, and even the ones who don't just stare straight ahead at their own computers with glazed looks in their eyes.

I remember I asked my dad once if he really liked working at my mom's tailor shop. It's not like he ever wanted to do that. In response, he told me a story about "one of the best days of my life before you girls were born." Turns out, it was just the day he quit his previous job in an office. I wasn't all that satisfied by that answer, but I have to admit, I kind of get a kick out of the thought that Dìyù is even a fraction as miserable for the netherworld beings to work in as it is for humans to have to go through.

"Should we try to talk to someone?" Kevin asks. He holds up the Staff of Mùlián, but I feel a little wary of alerting this entire workroom to our presence. They can't touch us while we're wielding the Staff, but they could alert White Boiler Suit that we're here. And if we have to use the Staff on them and they all try to rush for the front door at once, like the worker in the Third Court, we could get trampled.

"Maybe somewhere more private?" As I scan the room, I spot a futuristic-looking pod with glass walls. Inside is a single worker in a jade-green boiler suit, sitting in front of a laptop with a thermos in hand. I speed-walk over and slip inside. Kevin closes the door after he joins me, and immediately the noise from the rest of the office space becomes muffled.

"So I finally got around to looking at Penitent #12358's case. And get this, he was telling the truth this whole time," the Department of Records employee is saying. Engrossed on her laptop screen, she doesn't notice us enter the room. "He really *was* mixed up with a different Li Jianyu who was scheduled to die, and the unlucky sap got sent down here instead. Can you believe it?"

Since the pod is soundproof, the office demon isn't using headphones, so we can hear both halves of the conversation. "What a disaster!" says the person on the other end. "That's going to be so much paperwork."

"I *know*," the office demon groans, which, uh . . . would not be my reaction to such a horrific mistake. "I sent his file to the Fourth Court, but, ah, technically no one wronged him except whatever simpleton in Dìyù caused the error. So it's against policy for him to be there."

"Rough. So what's he gonna do?"

"Well, I don't think it can be helped now, so Mr. Hēi and Mr. Bái took him back to the First Court.

He'll have to wait it out there until he was originally fated to die and it's his turn before the Judge. It looks like he had a long, full life still ahead of him, so he'll be there for a while."

I feel like a volcano about to erupt. When the office demon reaches for her thermos, I lunge forward and spill it onto the carpet. It's super petty and I know it, but I don't care.

"Hey!" she cries, finally turning away from her screen. "What—" Her eyes widen when she sees me and Kevin, covered in blood and wielding the Staff of Mùlián. Before she can run for the exit, I snatch the Staff out of Kevin's hands and ring it. *CLANG!*

She lets out an ear-piercing shriek and falls right out of her chair, face-planting onto the carpet. The person on the other end of the line says, "Bibi? What was that?" But no one outside of the soundproof pod notices, the office workers all carrying on with their own tasks. The demon—Bibi—tries to bolt for the exit, but I ring the Staff again—*CLANG! CLANG!*—and she falls to the ground, her hands pressed tightly over her ears.

"Uh," Kevin says. "I'm picking up that you're really mad, and that's, like, valid, but today is actually not the first time I've seen someone torture a person in front of me, and I don't really like it."

"Well, that explains why you volunteered to come to the *literal torture labyrinth*," I retort. Kevin flinches, and I suddenly feel guilty. Kevin did come here to help me, and it's not right to yell at him for it. But then I remember the wrong Li Jianyu, and my fury returns with a vengeance.

I glare at the demon, then at the computer. Understanding immediately, she reaches out and ends the call. Then she throws her hands up in the air.

"I hung up! Now stop ringing that," she whines. "Who are you? What do you want?"

Even though I'm still simmering with rage at how little these people seem to care about an innocent person dying by mistake, it will have to wait. "I'm looking for my mom. Dawn Liu Huang. She's not supposed to be here, either." I can't help adding the last word, thinking of poor Li Jianyu, then realize she might misunderstand. "What I mean is, she's *alive*, but she was kidnapped and taken to Dìyù. Do you know where I can find her?"

"Didn't hear anything about it." Bibi adds quickly, "You can check my inbox if you don't believe me. I don't always open my memos, but I definitely would have if the subject line said anything about a live person in Dìyù."

My heart sinks. "This is the Department of Records. Wouldn't you be able to check? She hasn't been here long, only about ten days."

"*Pfft!* Do you know how many records we have to deal with? Over a hundred thousand people die every single day, and twenty percent of those are Chinese! In 'only' ten days, that's more than two hundred thousand records." It makes my blood boil to hear her talk about *hundreds of thousands of people dying* like that's just a really big stack of paperwork. "What you're describing is seriously abnormal. I don't even know what department would cover it. But it would have to go to the very top."

"You mean . . . Yama?"

Bibi nods. I picture the red-faced emperor on the joss paper dollars, maybe in an extra-fancy modern boiler suit with a tie. If the workers in Dìyù are all this terrible, what's the *boss* like? And unlike his underlings, we probably can't even bribe him to listen to us, considering his face is on the money.

But we can *make* him with the Staff. "Where can we find him?"

"His office is in the main administrative building right in the middle of Yōudū—that's the Fifth Court," Bibi whimpers. "Ground floor."

"Ground floor," I mutter, so I don't forget. "And speaking of Yama, you're not going to alert your boss that we just came here, because if you do, I'm going to tell him about Li Jianyu. Whose mix-up you're going to fix *immediately*. Even if you have to drop everything else to take care of it."

Bibi's bluish face becomes almost white. "Look, someone really messed up here, I'm not going to tell you otherwise. But I'm not just dropping his case because I'm heartless. He's already been in Dìyù for over a week. Even if I could get all the needed paperwork sorted out by the end of today"—as nervous as she is, she can't help snorting at this—"his family has probably already buried his body. He won't have anything to go back to."

"But . . ." For the first time, she looks really sorry, and to my horror, I think she's telling the truth. But it's just so unfair. Some careless office demon made a mistake, and then the rest of them didn't care enough to get it checked out immediately, so the wrong person had to die before his time and stay that way. And now his family has to live without him for no reason.

"Well, you can at least try," I say finally, even though I suspect but don't want to admit that there probably is nothing she can do. Still, I point at her laptop. As I tilt my head toward the screen, I see she was playing chess online, and I realize why she wasn't paying attention to us when we snuck inside.

"What the heck?" I blurt out, unable to hold back my disgust. "I don't wanna be all, 'Do your work!' But I mean . . . these are literally people's lives."

Suddenly, I'm so angry that I almost shake the Staff again, just to watch her suffer. But then I see Kevin, his eyes darting to the door, and I remind myself that Mom is waiting for me. She's been waiting for ten whole days.

Shaking my head, I walk out of the workstation, then out of the Department of Records. I don't realize how fast I'm going until I notice Kevin is struggling to keep up with me. We keep walking until we come across a large gray building bigger than any of the surrounding ones. Kevin glances at the Chinese characters on top.

"Yeah, this is the executive building," he announces.

I don't even bother to check whether the door is unlocked first, I simply slam the Staff of Mùlián against it. *CLANG!* There's a crashing noise as the door is sent flying through the hallway.

"Hey! Wait up!" Kevin shouts, running inside after me. An alarm blares through the halls, and when a demon in a black boiler suit comes rushing out, I run up to him.

"Where's King Yama?" The demon glares up at me, and I recognize him as the pint-sized narrator from the orientation video in the First Court.

"First of all, the boss is not a king anymore. He was stripped of his previous title after political reform in the supernatural realm." In contrast to his demented game show host energy in the orientation video, he now sounds like he's reciting from some handbook he was forced to memorize, all while rolling his eyes the entire time. "Yama's title is now the director of the Department of Infernal Affairs."

"How is that reform if literally the same person is still in charge and you just call him something different?"

"Exactly," Black Boiler Suit replies. It occurs to me that Bibi mentioned a Mr. Hēi and a Mr. Bái, or Mr. Black and Mr. White—that much Chinese I know. If the silent deaf white demon is Bái, that would make this one Hēi.

Mr. Hēi's eyes widen as he sees the Staff. "Hey, I remember that! That belonged to the more-enlightened-than-thou monk. How did you get that?"

"Doesn't matter. I need to talk to Yama. My mom was taken to Dìyù, but there's been a mistake. She's not supposed to be here—"

"That's what they all say. Didn't you watch the video?" Hēi sighs. "Look, kid, whatever your ma did in life to end up down here, she'll have to pay for it like a big girl, all right? So why don't you go home and play with your memes or whatever it is that children do for fun now."

I squeeze my hands around the Staff. But then Mr. Hēi adds, "But if you really want to talk to the boss, I *might* be able to tell you where he is." His eyes dart toward the handbag.

I resist the urge to groan. Sighing, I unzip the bag and take out a joss paper dollar. "Okay, I get it. You people like money. I'll give you ten thousand dollars if you tell me where your boss is. Heck, I'm in such a good mood, I'll give you *twenty* thousand dollars!" I pull out a second bank note, fighting the impulse to slap Mr. Hēi across the face with it.

Mr. Hēi looks over his shoulder, as if to make

sure no one is watching. Then he takes the cash. "All right," he says as he unzips a pocket on the side of his boiler suit and slips the dollars inside. "The boss's office is down the hall, second on your left. He's getting his daily, ah, treatment right now, so he might be a little cranky—"

Well, too bad for him. I take off down the hallway without even waiting for him to finish.

"You know, you could say thank you!" Hēi shouts, his voice echoing after me.

My heart thunders as I charge down the hall. I come to the second door on the left, which has a plaque reading YAMA, DIRECTOR OF THE DEPARTMENT OF INFERNAL AFFAIRS next to it.

"So, we're going to speak to the manager, huh?" Kevin remarks, panting. "Should we knock?"

I bang the Staff against the door. With a *CLANG!*, it falls off its hinges.

Heart pounding, I barge inside. Yama is sitting at his desk, holding a mug that reads NETHERWORLD'S BEST BOSS. The director has chin-length hair and a patchy dark beard, like if Keanu Reeves was full Asian, but I can recognize him as the king on the joss paper money from his deep red skin, which is just a shade lighter than his poorly fitting maroon silk pajamas. Look, I'm not trying to be a snob about pajamas, but I would expect the boss and former king of the netherworld to be able to afford a decent tailor.

And he isn't alone. Sitting across from him is the silent, white-suited demon, the yang to Mr. Hēi's yin, Mr. Bái.

My heart skips a beat when I see the silent demon, and nearly stops when his deathly white face snaps toward us. In an instant he gets to his feet, rising to his full, alarming height.

But before he can make a move, Yama holds up his hand. "These are the living children you were telling me about?" he rasps, addressing Mr. Bái. His voice sends chills down my spine: It's not strained so much as corroded, like his vocal cords have had holes poked in them. It reminds me of videos of former smokers that I've seen in health class, and I shudder with every syllable.

It embarrasses me a little how much my confidence evaporates as I realize the weapon I'm gripping is now useless. But I remind myself why I'm here. "I'm trying to find my mom. Dawn Liu Huang. Where is she?"

"How would I know?" Yama snaps. "You think I

remember every scumbag and screwup who ends up down here?"

"No, she's not dead—she was taken here, alive, by a yāoguài. She's alive just like us."

Yama just stares at me blankly, no hint in his bulging black eyes that he has any idea what I'm talking about. "All right, kid, I'll bite. When was this?" I tell him. "If your mom had entered Dìyù and been discovered, I would have heard of it by now," the director says. "But even if she could somehow escape the notice of the thousands of personnel that make up the Department of Infernal Affairs, why would she? Why wouldn't she just approach any of the administrative officials crawling all over this place and explain that she'd been abducted?"

I almost retort that Yama is way too confident in the integrity and dedication of his employees. But everything he's saying is exactly what I was thinking.

Yama sighs. "Anyway. You're not supposed to be here—not yet, anyway. Sorry for your loss."

He nods at Mr. Bái, who had been standing still, oblivious to our conversation. Yama signs with his hands, and Bái lurches forward toward us, his freakishly long fingers extended like grasping talons.

"No, you can't," I blurt out, frantic.

"Don't worry, he's not going to hurt you. You're not under my jurisdiction, so I couldn't technically punish you even if I wanted to. He's just going to take you straight to the exit."

But before Mr. Bái can grab us, Kevin swipes the NETHERWORLD'S BEST BOSS mug right out of Yama's hand. He flings the scorching hot liquid into Bái's white face, and the previously silent demon instantly falls backward, screeching in pain.

Kevin gapes in horror as Mr. Bái thrashes on the floor in agony, shiny silver liquid running down his face. "Oh my gosh! I'm so sorry!" Kevin babbles. "I didn't know—I mean, I was hoping it'd be hot, but I thought it'd be hot like coffee or tea! What is that? Is that metal?"

Yama gets to his feet. Before he can move toward us—or his phone to call for backup, or whatever it is he's thinking about doing—I ring the Staff of Mùlián. The director lets out a wail that feels like hot metal on my eardrums. He sinks to his knees as Kevin and I rush out the big hole where the door to Yama's office used to be.

"Great. How am I supposed to find my mom now?" I groan. My blood's boiling and the urge to throw something is overpowering. But I don't, because the thing I'm currently holding is the only thing keeping us from being kicked out of Dìyù and I have to keep going. But without any other leads, how am I supposed to find her?

"One Court at a time?" Kevin suggests.

The disappointment of not finding Mom here is still crushing. But Kevin's relentless positivity in the face of literal Hell doesn't baffle or annoy me like I might have thought.

"One Court at a time," I repeat. I can do that. When you put it like that, that doesn't sound too bad.

I unzip the handbag and take out the spool. "Do we go back to the elevator?" Kevin asks. "Or do you want to keep searching the Fifth Court?"

Before I can make up my mind, Yama's rasp comes on blaring over the intercom system, broadcasting his awful voice throughout the building.

"Department of Infernal Affairs, this is your director speaking. We are experiencing a security breach: Two living children have infiltrated Dìyù. They are armed with a highly dangerous magical staff, so netherworld personnel are advised not to engage.

"Which is why I am calling on the penitents of Dìyù with a once-in-an-afterlifetime offer. We have temporarily suspended the wind that normally steers you toward each of your torments, allowing you complete freedom of movement. Whoever among you can catch the intruders will have your sentences—no matter what your sins are—commuted."

"What does 'commuted' mean?" Kevin asks.

My blood runs cold. I don't know, either, but I think I can guess from the context.

"I'm not sure, but I think it means the punishments they were sentenced to in Dìyù will be reduced . . ."

By this time we've reached the front door of the executive building, and I think I'm right. Because less than five minutes after Yama's announcement, I can see through the open doorway that the Fifth Court is already surrounded by the condemned.

FOURTEEN
All Dìyù Breaks Loose

I look out the doorway at the horde of desperate dead people charging at the office building. Some are armed with makeshift weapons that they seem to have picked up from the other Courts: lunch trays from the food court, bricks from the walls that might have kept them out before we, uh, smashed them down.

Trying not to panic—which turns out to be a little like breaking an arm and "trying not to" hurt—I ring the Staff of Mùlián. Again, then again. *CLANG! CLANG! CLANG!* But it doesn't do any good: The dead people are still running toward the open door, not slowed or pushed back at all.

Dr. Hsu's words when Auntie Kathie tried to volunteer to go to Dìyù come back to hit me like a boomerang. Mùlián's Staff can repel supernatural beings. But the dead people in Dìyù aren't demons and they're not yet ghosts.

Oh.

Oh *no*.

"What do we do now? We're totally surrounded and our only weapon is useless against them!"

"Not our only weapon!" I look at Kevin, heart racing in anticipation, only to groan when he whips out his butterfly knife.

"Yeah, we're running." I turn around and run in the other direction just as the dead people swarm in through the building. Even with the door knocked down, some of them don't even bother to funnel through the single entrance, instead using their trays and other weapons to smash through the walls of the executive building and claw their way in.

"Great. *Great!*" I groan. "So not only do I have no idea where my mom is, I'm being chased by a guy with the word *racist* tattooed on his face."

"Wait, for real?" Kevin turns his head around. "Oh, dude, isn't that Wendell 'The Screwdriver' Milhaven? They made that really popular true crime documentary about him, *The Beast That Wore a Human Face*—"

I want to scream, but Thida always makes fun of

movie characters for doing that while running away from monsters and bad guys, because "it's a waste of oxygen and you need that to run."

"Kevin, I am begging you, please do not tell me anything more about this movie."

"*Ow!* What was that?" Kevin rubs the back of his head, and a few seconds later, I feel a sharp pain in the back of my skull, too. I look over my shoulder and see that a dead woman has fashioned a slingshot by tying together chopsticks with a plastic wrapper. She fishes out a single grain of rice from the bowl at her feet, places it in her mouth, and spits out a little metal ball, which she then proceeds to fire up in the slingshot and launch toward us.

"Hey, that's pretty cool!" Kevin says.

"It would be cooler if she wasn't aiming them at us."

I turn to the side wall and smash it down with the Staff. We make a run for it, the penitents following after us.

"What do we do?" Kevin asks.

I try to think of something, but my mind goes blank. For all I'd complained about the Guilds being useless, the truth is I'd put all my hopes on having the Staff of Mùlián to protect us. But now we're being pursued by people we can't shoo away with the Staff, and now that we've been turned into two running get-out-of-Dìyù-free cards, we won't be able to bribe them with netherworld money, either.

I smash down the door of the adjacent office building. But before Kevin can run in after me, a penitent comes charging out of nowhere and tackles him to the floor.

"Kevin!" I watch in horror as he tries to get to his feet, only for the penitent to grab his leg and pull him back down again. The man is built like a school bus, and he flings Kevin around like a rag doll. Before I even have time to think about it, I find myself running forward and swinging the Staff of Mùlián at the dead guy's bald head.

"Ow!" The penitent spins around to face me, revealing the word RACIST inked in huge block letters across his angry face. And I realize with horror that the large, furious man I just whacked in the head is Wendell Milhaven, aka The Screwdriver, aka The Beast That Wore a Human Face.

But then he falls over, clutching his knee and howling with pain. Kevin stands up, panting and gripping the metal handle from the door I had smashed moments ago. He gives me a thumbs-up, a nervous smile on his face.

"N-nice," I pant. My heart is ticking so fast, like a time bomb in the final seconds before it blows up or the heroes disable it. "For a moment there, I really thought I was gonna die."

"Me too!" Kevin says. I grab his hand to go, but then I see more penitents are heading our way.

"Quick! Give me the spool!" Kevin says. I don't understand what he's thinking, but I hand him the tangled mass of thread from my pocket. He wraps it around the door handle, then swings it toward the penitents as they rush forward.

"Oh, *nice*," I say, watching in astonishment as the door handle shoots into someone's chest, causing him to double over in pain. Kevin pulls the handle back and throws it again, but since the thread is so tangled, it can't go very far, and his aim isn't great. And more penitents are coming.

"There's too many of them," I say, frantic. Even if the thread wasn't tangled and Kevin's specific Warrior skill was the art of using this exact random weapon, we'd be overwhelmed by sheer numbers. This isn't an action movie where the hero is surrounded by bad guys but they all only come up to fight one at a time just to be polite.

I clutch the Staff as they close in, even though it's useless against them except as a big stick. But then I remember something else Mùlián's Staff can do.

"Hey, all the Courts are stacked on top of each other, right?" I ask Kevin.

Kevin picks up what I'm putting down. "Are you thinking we can smash through the floor again? Like we did in the blood pool?"

"Yeah. But do you think it's a good idea? What if we fall into, like, a pot of boiling oil or something?"

"Oh. Uh. Shoot." Kevin furrows his brow, considering our options. But then I hear a grunt, and then to my horror I see that The Screwdriver has gotten to his feet and is charging toward us, screaming.

"Go for it," Kevin says quickly. He grabs on to my arm, and I raise the Staff, then bring it down onto the floor beneath my feet.

CLANG! Cracks appear in the floor, then spread across the white tiles like the surface of a frozen pond breaking. And then . . . we're falling.

"Whoa!" Kevin squeezes me tighter as we fall, and despite my pounding heartbeat, I exhale in relief when I look up and see that the penitents are still standing in the Fifth Court.

But then I look down at the Sixth Court and see that we're plummeting straight down toward a mountain in the middle of a dense forest. Both the trees and the mountain are covered with hundreds of incredibly sharp swords and knives.

FIFTEEN

Hanging by a Thread

"AHHHHHHH!" we scream as we fall down toward near-certain doom. There are so many blades, there's pretty much no chance we don't land on one.

Frantic, I swing the Staff of Mùlián like it's a fishing rod, trying to maneuver it so the brass rings can catch on the ceiling lights hanging above the hallway in the Fifth Court. But I miss: We've fallen too far down, and the Staff isn't long enough to reach it.

"Oh, come on!" I yell, my voice echoing off the mountain.

But then my hands twitch, wanting to leap to the red string pendant—and I remember that we have a magic string that can go on indefinitely. I look over at Kevin. To my relief, he's still holding on to the door handle with the thread tied to it. I take the handle and tell the spool, "Find something to hold on to."

Kevin takes the tangled mass of thread and tries his best to tie it around our waists, binding us together. I spin it around and then let go.

The door handle flies through the air, and despite all the entanglements, the thread continues to extend even as we fall. I hold my breath for what seems like forever until I hear a *CLANG!* I feel a tug on my wrist, and then the string goes tight and then . . . we stop falling.

"It worked!" I release my breath, relieved to not be Evie Mei Huang satay.

"So, uh . . ." Kevin looks down as we swing slowly back and forth, our bodies pressed together. "Now what?"

I look down at the forest of swords below us, feeling both relieved and queasy at how much closer we are to them than I had realized. But we don't seem to be in immediate danger of plummeting to our doom. The single thread shouldn't be able to support our weight, but it feels as secure and strong as a rope. It reminds me of how Thida told me that spider thread is stronger than steel, which messes with my head.

"The thread can run infinitely, right?" I say. "We can roll it down and climb down it until we reach the ground."

I drop the spool, and sure enough, the tangled red thread grows longer and longer as it falls toward the ground. But before we can begin our descent, I spot figures moving in between the swords. My stomach churns as a little old lady pulls out a sword from the mountain and uses it to hack a branch off a tree, which she then proceeds to swing at us.

"Hey! Stop! Go away!"

We're at least twenty feet up from the ground and the old woman is not very tall; she has to jump just to try and hit us. It's kind of funny—until a group of dead people materialize from the forest and gather in a circle below us, all swinging tree branches at us like we're a piñata.

"Ow!" A branch scratches my shin. When I try to wave the Staff menacingly at them, I lurch to the side and accidentally elbow Kevin in the face. Before I can apologize, I hear a distant *clink* of metal and feel another tug on the string. My heart sinks as I realize the door handle came loose from whatever it was caught on when I tried to swing out of the penitents' way.

"We can't move around too much or we'll yank the handle right off," I say in a hushed whisper. If we do that, we're all but guaranteed to fall. But *not* moving makes it that much easier for the penitents to hit us.

Except one dead guy isn't swinging tree branches at us. He's sitting on the ground, hugging his knees and looking deep in thought. "Have you tried turning it off and turning it back on," he says as he rocks back and forth, apparently to himself. Because of the mountain, I can hear his voice echoing even from the ground. Then he shouts, "Have you tried turning it off and turning it back on!" He leaps into the air, and the other penitents stop swinging their branches at us to stare at him.

"Eh?" another penitent grunts.

The man explains, "I was IT support when I was alive. And at least a third of the calls I got could be fixed just by turning the computer off and turning it back on again."

"The nerd's lost his mind in here," someone else mutters.

The other penitents turn back toward us, shaking their heads. But IT Support points at us and shouts, "We're in the afterlife! Every time we die in here, we come back to life so we can be tortured all over again. Instead of trying to capture them, we can just *kill them* and *then* hand them over to Yama. They'll come back to life, just like the computers!"

The rest of the penitents stare blankly at him for a

few moments. But then to my horror they start murmuring and nodding.

"Oh no. No, no, no, no," I mutter, my heart pounding desperately as the penitents start pulling out knives from the surrounding trees. The gravity of the situation dawns on me: If they *kill us*, we'll be stuck in Dìyù. And so will Mom.

"Okay, on the count of three!" shouts IT Support, his sweaty face flushed and energized from everyone listening to his plan. His ingenious plan to *just kill us*. As the penitents start forming a circle, knives at the ready, my palms start to sweat uncontrollably.

"One!" IT Support yells. But then he yells "Ow!" as one of the other penitents smacks him upside the head. "Hey, what was that for?"

"You're not the boss of me, nerd," the other penitent sneers. IT Support scowls.

"Oh, shoot, they're really going to kill us!" Kevin blurts out. For the first time this entire unbelievable day, I see genuine panic in his eyes. He unzips the handbag, still dangling from my arm.

"What are you doing?" I yell as he reaches for the painting of Auntie Kathie's apartment. "If we go back, we'll have to go through the first six Courts all over again."

For a moment it becomes silent, until IT Support's voice echoes, "Two!" below us.

"You can't find your mom, either, if they kill you," Kevin says quietly. "Well, I guess you could, but then you'd be dead, so it would be kinda different."

IT Support shouts, "THREE!"

We end our stare-off to look down, and my heart stops as the penitents all reach back and fling their knives and swords up in the air toward us . . .

. . . but then, because this isn't an action movie and these are all just random people who were less than shining examples of humanity and not trained projectile-throwers, the knives and swords fall back down without coming anywhere near us.

I'm so relieved, I start laughing nervously. But moments later I feel a tug. I look down and see that the red thread is still falling—and the old woman who had initially tried to hit us with the tree branch has noticed it, too.

"They're tied to it!" She yanks on the thread wildly, as if she's ringing a bell. But the string is still secure around our waists, and we don't fall.

For a moment, she looks up at us, then at the thread dangling above her head. Then she grips on to it and begins climbing up.

She doesn't look like she should be fast, but she shoots up the string like a cat dashing up a tree. Soon the other penitents are climbing the slender but sturdy thread after her, knives in their mouths.

"Oh, shoot!" Kevin pulls out his butterfly knife. My free hand had been tugging at my red string necklace from Mom, and suddenly, I remember what Monk said about Weaver thread.

"Wait, don't cut it!" I protest as Kevin successfully opens the knife without flipping it. "If you break the thread, it'll lose its enchantment, and then it won't be able to hold our weight."

Kevin doesn't say anything, but exhales in horror as the implications of this sink in. But the penitents are almost halfway up the thread now, and some are literally armed to the teeth.

"Okay," he says, swallowing. I brace myself for him to reach for the painting again, but he doesn't. "Uh. Shoot, uh, what else do I have on me?"

"Like to throw at them?" I look around. "Well, we're surrounded by weapons, but we'd have to swing toward the swords, and uh, I really don't think we should swing toward the swords."

"Oh, I got it!" Kevin reaches back into the pocket of his hoodie and pulls out his laser pointer. He aims it downward and flashes the green laser beam right into the old woman's eye. She yelps and drops the knife in her mouth. He then proceeds to shine the light into the eyes of the other penitents, holding it until they close or cover their eyes. Because they're all dangling below us in a straight line and can't move out of the way, he has no problem hitting each of them in turn.

"Nice." I had been skeptical about how effective this would be, but the penitents' movement up the thread slows to a crawl. None of them really look hurt, but several blink repeatedly and look disoriented. Others just close their eyes but have to fumble their way up the thread to avoid colliding with the penitents in front of them. The laser even penetrates IT Support's glasses, causing him to cry out.

"Do you have a cat?" I ask Kevin, trying to break the tension a little.

"No, but I had an Uncle Gunnar who was put under house arrest for aiming lasers at airplane pilots."

But the laser pointer only slows them down. It doesn't stop them. They continue to climb up, their eyes closed or averted, and we still have no other way to reach the ground.

"Can you try pointing at their hands?" I suggest. Kevin aims the laser away from IT Support's other eye and toward his fingers around the thread. But if it hurts his skin at all, it's not nearly enough to make him lose his grip.

"It's not doing anything," Kevin says.

The old woman screams, "Enough of this!" and begins dashing up the thread like a spider monkey, her eyes shut. Kevin frantically aims the laser pointer directly into her face, but she just keeps climbing up. When she's within grabbing distance of us, I kick at her, but with alarming reflexes she catches my foot and grabs on to it, her eyes still closed.

"Hey! Get off of me!" I try to kick her away, but even though she's tiny, her grip is like iron. I try to whack her with the Staff, but quickly regret it because she grips on to it, hoisting herself up until she's eye level with me. Her face is covered with dozens of wounds, as if she's been stabbed over and over.

"Got you!" she growls. For a moment, I consider whether I should drop the Staff, but before I can think about it any longer, she's reached out with her free hand to grab the front of my shirt. Kevin turns to help me, but she knocks the laser pointer out of his hand.

Seeing this, the other penitents quickly scramble up the thread. Even if we knock the old woman off the string, there's no way we can fight off everyone.

I flail as the old woman tries to untie the mass of thread from around our waists with her teeth. Thankfully, it's so tangled that she can't, nor does it come loose when she tries to pull it. But she doesn't let go even as both Kevin and I try to push her away with the Staff and his hands. Grimacing, she jerks her head downward and sees the line of other penitents farther down the thread. "You fools! How am I supposed to get down now?"

The penitents suddenly stop climbing. An awkward silence follows as they realize the situation they've gotten themselves into.

"Just pass them down the line!" IT Support calls out from below. "We can relay them to the bottom and then climb down."

The penitents murmur in agreement. But then someone cries out, "But how do we know the person at the bottom won't run off with them?"

"Why would they do that? Yama didn't say only one person could get the reward," IT Support says. "Why can't we all turn them in together and all go free?"

"I was in the First Court with the woman at the bottom! I saw her trial!" another person cries out. "She ran out on her aging parents! How can we trust that she won't run off on us?"

That logic doesn't totally check out to me, but it seems to give the penitents pause. As they argue among themselves, yelling over each other to be heard, the echoes of their voices reverberate off the mountain, blending together in a chorus of angry shouting. On instinct I reach up to cover my ears and nearly drop the Staff.

Suddenly I get an idea. I don't think ringing the Staff could cause an avalanche—I'm pretty sure that only works in movies. But as loud as it is on its own, the echo must be overwhelming.

"Cover your ears," I tell Kevin.

Then I swing the Staff.

CLANG! Then: *CLAAAAAAAANG!* Because I'm holding the Staff, I can't cover my own ears. The echo of the metal rings makes my ears ring, too. The old woman nearly topples over; she catches herself in time, but her iron grip on my shirt loosens. I grit my teeth, but even though it hurts my eardrums, I swing the Staff again. And again.

CLANG! CLANG! CLAAAAAAAANG! CLANG! CLAAAAAAAANG!

Screams, followed by echoes of screams. When I look down, I see that several of the penitents have lost their hold on the thread and are plummeting straight toward the ground.

Out of desperation, the old woman reaches out for the Staff, as do several of the other penitents dangling below us. But I manage to maneuver the Staff out of the way in time, and the movement creates an echoing *CLAAAAAANG!* The old woman as well as all the other penitents reaching out toward it lose their balance and are sent flying into the sword-covered mountain or the knife-covered trees or straight to the ground far below us.

Kevin peers down at the now-empty thread below us. "Uh. Are they . . ."

"I think so, but you heard what the IT guy said. They won't be for long. We need to go." And with that, we scramble down the thread before they can come back to "life."

Once we're safely on the ground, I untie the thread around our waists, then pull. The door handle falls somewhere in the forest of sword-covered trees, but I do my best to tie the rest of the thread back around the spool. Then I look around at all the bodies lying motionless on the ground. Despite my relief, I can't help but grimace at the sight.

"They'll come back to life," Kevin says quietly, as if he can hear my thoughts.

"No, they won't." They might come back, but they'll still be dead. That's literally why they're here.

But that's not my problem right now. "Mom?" I shout. My voice echoes off the mountain and throughout the entire Sixth Court. No one answers—I'd hear it because it'd echo back.

"She's not here, either." I didn't really think she would be—all the swords on the trees would make the Sixth Court too dangerous to stay in for too long. But every time we go through another Court and she's still not here, I feel the bitter sting of disappointment.

"One Court at a time," I murmur, steadying myself. To the spool, I say, "Take us to the Seventh Court." Once more, I tie the end of the thread to my finger and let the spool fall. It hits the ground rolling, and we continue after it through Dìyù.

SIXTEEN

There's No Place like Hell

Before we leave the Sixth Court, we steal white sweatsuits from two of the dead people on the ground. We're still carrying the Staff of Mùlián, so it's not a foolproof disguise, but at least we'll be a little less recognizable on sight.

Kevin also tries to grab a sword before we go, but they turn out to be literal double-edged swords—to stick into the trees as well as outward for stabbing—and he ends up leaving them. Instead he takes a knife and uses the string of his hoodie to tie it around the top of the Staff, turning it into the Spear of Mùlián. He might not be conventionally "good" at "fighting," but I have to hand it to him, he's pretty resourceful.

The spool leads us to a well in the middle of the forest. It rolls in and falls straight down, and I untie it from my finger and to a nearby branch so we can climb down. To my relief, no mobs are waiting to attack us when our feet touch down onto the Seventh Court. In fact, it appears to be completely deserted.

"Where is everybody?" I mean, I'm not complaining, but it's kind of unsettling.

"Maybe they all went to find us after Yama made his offer?" Kevin suggests. He points his spear up at the ceiling, to indicate where we just came from. That makes some sense to me, but considering all the Courts are designed like mazes with twisting passageways, I'm surprised there wouldn't be more people who are still trying to find their way out to get to us. I keep my guard up as I scan the area.

As we enter the maze, the phone light shines on a group of tiny figures looking out at me from a dead end. I almost jump, but then I realize it's not a person: It's a life-sized cutout of a group of children with big rosy cheeks, all smiling and pointing left.

"Well, that's totally not suspicious at all," I mutter. But when I look left, I notice another sign. This one is in multiple languages, so I can read it without Kevin having to translate:

THIS WAY TO THE TOWER OF VIEWING HOME
SEE YOUR FAMILIES AND FRIENDS ONE MORE TIME

"Okay, that's got to be a trap, right?" says Kevin. "Why would Dìyù allow people to see their families again? That doesn't seem like torture."

As I look at the sign, I flash back to Āh Mā's birthday a couple of years ago. The Avalon Library has a Memory Lab with all this equipment so you can digitize old family photos and home movies and stuff, and my dad spent weeks converting all their old family albums. He was really proud of it, thinking she would be thrilled to have photos from her childhood and her younger days to share on Facebook with her friends like old people love to do. And she did seem to love it when we showed them to her. But as we browsed through the albums, which included photos of her parents and Āh Gong and one of her brothers who isn't alive anymore, she became really sad.

At the time I remembered feeling terrible for my dad, who had spent so much time and been so excited about this gift for his mom. But after what I've been through the past ten days, I think I can understand how my grandma felt, too. When you're drowning in blood and running up mountains covered with knives, you probably don't have much time to think about the families you left behind. At the same time, who could resist the temptation to see how their families are doing after they're gone?

"No, I think it is torture," I say quietly. A subtle brutal kind of torture, one that the dead might not even realize *is* torture until they go there. I shudder, but then I get another thought.

"Do you think my mom might have gone to the Tower?" If she's made it this far, it would be a pretty good place to camp out while waiting to be rescued. She wouldn't be in danger, and she could also see us while she's there.

I squeeze my red string pendant, suddenly overwhelmed. It's a nice thought, that she really was watching over us all this time and that's not just a dumb thing my Auntie Diane said. But then I think about not sleeping for a week straight, and Mona Li sobbing into the night, and Dad smiling through the pain, and I feel a sharp pain in my chest, like falling onto a mountain of swords, at how agonizing these past ten days would havc been for Mom, too.

Kevin looks again at the sign, THE TOWER OF VIEWING HOME. I remember how he reached for the painting in the Sixth Court, and my stomach drops like when we were plummeting toward the swords.

I know what he's thinking. Can we really find my

mom now, with the spool unable to lead us directly to her and all the desperate dead people in Dìyù out to get us? But all I can think about is the time I got up at 4:00 A.M. to watch *Everything Everywhere All at Once*, when Mom suddenly walked inside. Apparently she'd left the house in the middle of the night to be with Auntie Kathie after The Gambler called her again to say he was "really sorry this time." But instead of getting mad, Mom took me to the 24-hour diner across the street and we had a very early breakfast, just the two of us.

She didn't tell Dad about it, because he would have freaked out that she could've been attacked going out in the middle of the night. But well, Mom doesn't like being told what to do. I once told her she's the most arrogant person I've ever met, and it's true, but what I never told her is that she's also the funniest. I almost snorted milkshake out of my nose as she told me all about the wild weekend that Auntie Kathie broke up with her boyfriend on the limo ride to her senior prom, so Mom went to pick her up and they ended up going on a spontaneous road trip. As we were sneaking back into the apartment at just before 7:00 A.M., I remember thinking it was nice to know that someday I could just call my mom in the middle of the night after a bad breakup and she'd come over. I don't know if I'd do it, because Mom would definitely tell me *I told you so*, but there was something really nice about knowing that I could. Even if Mom did tell me I was super grounded the next morning.

I can't give up, but it isn't really fair to make Kevin keep going now. He did volunteer to come into the torture labyrinth, but that was when he thought the Staff of Mùlián would protect us. Being chased by mobs of desperate condemned souls throwing bricks and knives at us isn't what he signed up for.

"Hey, Kevin?" I say softly. "Do . . . do you want to leave? If you do, that's okay." I really don't want him to go, and not just because that means I'll have to find my mom alone. But if he goes, I'll just have to find Mom myself. Somehow.

But to my surprise, Kevin shakes his head. "No. Let's keep going."

"Are you sure? You really don't have to." It occurs to me that I've been doing that a lot lately—telling people they don't have to help me when I want them to. Is that what growing up is? Because it sucks and I hate it.

"No, I mean it," Kevin insists. "I've been thinking about how my grandma and my Uncle Gunnar and, like, half the Warriors keep telling my mom to give up on hunting the Zodiac Killers because it won't bring my dad back. But this is different, because we are going to bring your mom back."

I wasn't expecting that at all, and it hits me harder than I would have guessed. I bite back a lump forming in my throat. "Thanks, Kevin" is all I can say to that.

We follow the creepy sign into the maze, Kevin brandishing his makeshift spear. But we don't encounter any more dead people. The maze is full of twists and turns, with more cardboard cutouts pointing us down dead ends and back out of dead ends and into increasingly complicated loop-de-loops. But the only torture here seems to be that it's an unnecessarily prolonged and frustrating way to the Tower—and it works, because I definitely am getting frustrated.

"Is this even the fastest way to the Tower?" I mutter.

"Does this even lead *to* the Tower?" Kevin says, and I stop in my tracks. That does sound like something Dìyù would come up with: promising its penitents a chance to see home again, then sending them down an endless series of dead ends.

I tell the spool, "Take us to the Tower of Viewing Home." To my relief, it immediately falls to the ground and begins rolling. So now we know for sure there *is* a Tower. After ten days, I hope my mom will have been able to find it, too.

"Looks like that's a yes," I say, and we continue walking through the Seventh Court. We still don't run into anyone, and Kevin eventually loosens his grip on the Staff/spear. I turn around each pointing cardboard cutout we pass, though, to misdirect anyone who comes down looking for us.

The murals get more ominous the farther we go. At first they just seem like sentimental scenes of ordinary life and events, like wall-sized greeting cards: a wedding, a house. But then I notice there's text in different languages with the most depressing clickbait captions ever, like YOU WON'T BELIEVE THE LOSER YOUR GRANDDAUGHTER MARRIED! and WHAT THEY DID WITH ALL THE MONEY YOU SPENT YOUR WHOLE LIFE WORKING SO HARD TO EARN WILL SHOCK YOU!

That first one reminds me, Auntie Kathie must be worried about me. I check the handkerchief, which I had completely forgotten about after the demon worker in the food court spotted us. My heart leaps when I see that Auntie Kathie had replied to my message, meaning my attempt at needle-writing worked: underneath my clumsy *we r here* are the words *ok! be safe!* in hot-pink thread. At first I'm a little surprised at such a short message from my chatty aunt, but since the handkerchief has such limited space, I guess it makes sense that she doesn't want to spam us with messages unless it's really important.

"Oh hey, she replied!" Kevin says. "Do you want to tell your aunt what Yama told the people in Dìyù? Maybe someone in the Guilds will know what to do."

I know he's right, but part of me doesn't want to. If they can't help us, it'll just make Auntie Kathie even more worried than she already is. She'd probably just tell us to give up and come home, and that's not an option.

But I have to admit the situation is not looking great, and if there *is* something they could tell us that could help save Mom, we have to ask. "I guess it can't hurt," I say reluctantly.

I pick up my makeshift hairpin needle, and after thinking a little bit about how to say this with as few characters as possible, sew into the handkerchief: *yama sent dead ppl after us. staff cant stop them*, then a crooked question mark. It's to the point, but I think it's clear enough.

Five seconds later, more letters stitch themselves along the borders of the handkerchief. My aunt clearly isn't bothering to make her stitches perfectly neat like my mom does, but she sews her hot-pink words remarkably fast. *And* they're still more even than mine.

come home

NOW

Well, I guess it was worth a try. I'm debating whether it would be ruder to leave my aunt on read or reply just to say *no*, but then I see that another message has materialized. "Hey, Kevin?" I say, handing the handkerchief to him. "My aunt has a message for you."

"Oh, cool!" Kevin reads it aloud: *"Kev, I found who your red thread is tied to. You kept your promise, I'll keep mine."*

Wow. So my aunt's trying to get to me through Kevin. His eyes widen, and for a moment, I'm afraid it just might work.

"Hey, you know what this means?" Kevin says.

I swallow. "What?"

Kevin breaks into a grin. "The red string of fate means I'm destined to be with this person no matter what, right? And now that I know I have one, I know it's not my fate to die in Dìyù."

For a moment, I'm at a loss for words. "I—I guess not," I say finally. Kevin picks up the Staff of

Mùlián, still grinning from ear to ear, and we continue walking.

The Tower of Viewing Home is hideous.

When I read the sign, I was picturing the Tower like a traditional Chinese pagoda with multiple tiers and elegant curving roofs. But the building in front of us is a big, imposing, ugly block, an unpainted concrete monolith that quite literally stands in stark contrast to the cheerfully depressing murals that adorn the rest of the Seventh Court.

As we approach the Tower, it at last clicks into place why this Court was empty. Strewn all around the base of the building are motionless bodies. When I look up at the Tower and see the single staircase winding around the entire ugly thing, no guardrails anywhere in sight, it doesn't take Batman to deduce what must have happened. Everyone at the Tower must have rushed to get down the single set of stairs after Yama made his announcement on the intercom, causing a stampede that sent them all plummeting over the edge or tumbling down the steps, and then . . . *SPLAT*.

For a moment, we stand in silence, looking at all the unmoving bodies. Even though they're literally all out to get us, the grim sight still makes me sick. If they were on the Tower of Viewing Home, they must have just been looking at their families, or waiting in line to, when Yama's announcement came on. There's something so sad about that.

But I don't have time to take a moment of silence on their behalf. I run past the bodies and charge my way up the stairs. At the top of the Tower is an observation deck encircled by viewing devices.

I take a moment to catch my breath, only realizing for the first time that I'm out of it from climbing up all those stairs. My relief not to have to run from and/or fight off any more penitents instantly sours to crushing disappointment as I look around the empty observation deck.

"Mom?" I call out as I circle the deserted platform again and again. No response. She isn't here, either. I look out over the platform at the Seventh Court. From here I can see the entire maze, and aside from the pile-up of bodies around the foot of the Tower, the place is completely empty.

"I'm sorry," Kevin says softly, and I almost jump.

In my rush to race up the Tower, I hadn't even realized he was right behind me.

"Three more Courts to go," I say, my voice as flat as a pancake. I turn to make the trip back down the stairs, but then stop and stare at the viewing device closest to me.

I'd been so focused on bringing Mom home, I hadn't even realized how much I miss Dad and Mona Li until just now. Even though I've only been in Dìyù for a few hours at the most, I've spent so much of that time worrying about my mom, and suddenly I feel desperate to see the rest of my family.

I plant both feet in front of the viewing device and look through. My heart catches in my throat when I see our apartment living room. Dad is pacing back and forth and talking on the phone, just like he was when I left him.

I've been knocking his not-at-all reassuring fake smile a lot, but I'm starting to think I was complaining too much. When I see the look of total raw anguish on his face without me or Mona Li around to pretend for, however unconvincingly, I feel like I've been stabbed in the heart. He's clearly making an effort to speak quietly, and my little sister is wailing in the background. But his words are somehow crystal clear.

"I haven't told Evie yet. She went out with her friend and I don't want to call them just to ruin her birthday. I can tell her when she comes home."

Huh? What is he talking about?

Dad becomes quiet, and I wait for him to continue speaking. After what feels like forever, he continues, his voice shaky, "Yeah, I can still identify her from her clothes. I'd know Dawn's work anywhere."

What?!?!

"I'm going to go check on Mona Li. I know I've been saying that this doesn't really change anything, and it'd be nice for the girls to have some closure at least, but I think—I think she was holding out hope."

Dad pauses and presses his hand to his mouth. He's fighting back tears and the tears are winning as he says, his voice cracking, "I can't say this in front of Evie and Mona Li, but I keep thinking it should have been me instead of Dawn. She'd be able to hold it together for them instead of falling apart."

"Hey, is everything okay?" Kevin says. My head is spinning, and my legs are wobbling like they're made of jelly.

Dad was talking like Mom's body was *found*. But

that doesn't make any sense, because she never died. She was taken to Dìyù . . .

The scene abruptly changes to show Auntie Kathie's living room. Monk is tied to a chair, surrounded by the Elders. My aunt, ominously, is nowhere to be seen, but I can hear a woman screaming in the background. I've spent the past week listening to my sister cry herself to sleep every single night, and I've heard all kinds of horrendous shrieks in Dìyù. But the sound of my aunt's wails still makes my blood run cold. It'd be wrong to call it hysterical. It's . . . animal-like.

The sound of a phone alarm goes off, and Dr. Fang taps her screen to silence it. The leader of the Alchemists' face is hard as she glowers at the yāoguài. "All right, the truth serum should be in full effect by now. Thank the heavens, because you have a *lot* of explaining to do. Who sent you after Límíng?"

Monk blows Dr. Fang a raspberry. But then he sighs. "No one."

The Elders exchange confused glances. "No one?" Dr. Hsu repeats.

"What are you, an echo? No one. I never took her to Dìyù, either. I made up the entire story. Word in the supernatural community was that the head of the Weavers was missing along with the Spindle of Fate.

I thought if I convinced her kid that she'd been taken there, she would give me her string and I could track the Spindle down."

I suddenly can't breathe. I massage my temple, trying to stay calm even though I feel like I was when I was sinking beneath the blood.

"But why would you do that?" Dr. Hsu asks. "Only Dawn can use the Spindle."

Even though the yāoguài's shoulders are tied to the chair, he manages a shrug with his tail. "*I* know that, but I figured I could make a fortune selling it to someone who doesn't."

My head is spinning so bad, and I'm vaguely aware of Kevin putting a hand on my shoulder and leading me away from the edge of the Tower, like he's afraid I might lose my balance and fall off.

To my surprise, Thida steps forward then. I couldn't see her between Wood and Fire Elders because she's so tiny. What's she still doing here? She holds up the scroll, which unfurls to reveal my mother's message in needle-writing. "What about this, then?"

"I hired a seamstress to stitch that," Monk replies. "It was easier than trying to fake her handwriting without opposable thumbs. I searched the shop after

Dawn went missing and found notes she wrote for her kids. I lifted the 'P.S.' straight from those notes so Evie would be sure it was her."

"So, you have *no* idea where Evie's mom is? You just told her you did so you could find the Spindle?" Thida says. "Why tell such a complicated fake story about her being in Dìyù?"

Without missing a beat, Monk answers truthfully, "I thought it was funny."

I've never seen Thida really, really angry before. It transforms her entire face, making her look like some kind of demon herself. But I'm too confused to be angry.

The Elders exchange glances. "So Límíng *isn't* in Dìyù?" Dr. Fang says. "For heaven's sake! Is she even still alive?"

"The daughter," Cyrus Lie says quietly. "We need to get her and Kevin out of Dìyù. Where's Kathie?"

Like an actress right on cue, my aunt bursts into the living room then. Her hands are shaking, and she looks almost dazed.

"I . . . I just got a call. Dawn—" Her voice cracks, and she buries her face in her hands as she wails, "Th-they just found her body."

No.

No, no, no, no.

I can't have come all this way just to find out that Mom has actually been dead the whole time. My mom can't really be dead; nothing looks the same.

But then I remember all the murals in this awful place, taunting the dead with their loved ones' terrible fates and poor life choices. The Seventh Court doesn't let condemned souls see their loved ones because it feels sorry for them: It does that because it's *psychological torture*.

This is all an illusion. Dìyù is tricking me into thinking my mom really is dead in order to torment me.

Slowly, I take two steps back away from the viewfinder. Kevin is waiting for me, his eyes wide.

"Hey, is everything okay?"

"Yeah," I say, a little too quickly. Kevin opens his mouth, clearly not buying this at all. "Okay, no. But it doesn't really matter."

I don't tell him what I saw, and he doesn't press me. But as I turn away, eager to leave the Tower, I can't help but shoot a glance back toward the viewing device, unable to erase what I saw from my memory.

SEVENTEEN

NOT THE BEASTS!

I'm still shaken, but we have to get moving. We still have three Courts of Dìyù left to search, and I'd rather go through ten more than go back home without Mom.

I take out the spool and let it fall again. After nearly face-planting onto hundreds of swords, I think I'll pass on any more shortcuts straight through the ground except as a last resort.

"Take us to the Eighth Court." We follow the spool as it plunks down the stairs and off, then around, the Tower of Viewing Home.

It leads us to another staff elevator on the other side of the Tower. No one's inside, with the Dìyù staff having taken cover, but the Eighth Court probably won't be as empty.

"Hey, are you sure you're okay?" Kevin asks as I

press the *4* button third from the bottom for the Eighth Court. That hasn't gotten any less annoying. "You haven't seemed the same since the Tower. Did you see your family? Is everything okay at home?"

This kid is not as clueless as I'd dismissed him as at first, but suddenly I find myself wishing he were. "Oh. Yeah, I did, but it's okay." When Kevin doesn't seem convinced by this, I say, "I mean, it isn't true anyway. It's all torture, right? So it's not worth thinking about."

Kevin furrows his brow, absorbing this. "Yeah, that makes sense," he says finally. "I'm sorry you had to see . . . whatever it was you saw, though."

That makes two of us. "Did you look through the viewer?" I hadn't really been thinking about it because I was so shocked by what the Tower was showing me, but Kevin must have wanted to see his mom, too.

"Yeah, I did. Like you said, it's not worth thinking about."

Considering the third or fourth thing Kevin told me when we met is that his mom has killed nearly a dozen people, and one of the next things after that was about his urological problems (well, his "friend's," but, like, come on), the fact that there's something he might *not* be willing to share stuns me. We ride the rest of the elevator in silence. Even though it's just a single flight down, it feels longer until the doors open and we step out into the Eighth Court.

There are colorful murals here, too, these ones showing cartoon animals. They wouldn't look out of place in a preschool or a nursery, until I look closer and see that the cute tigers and wolves and bears are chasing dead people dressed in white. One ominous wall has graffiti written on it that reads simply NOT THE BEES!

It's not hard to figure out what the torture in this Court is. "This seems like a bad place to be drenched in blood," I mutter. Sure enough, ten seconds later we follow the spool down a corner and find ourselves staring at a bull the size of a tank, with horns as sharp as knives. Also, the bull is on fire?!

Snorting smoke from its nostrils, the flaming bull charges toward us. But Kevin rings the Staff, and as soon as it's resounded a single *CLANG!*, the bull stops in its tracks, turns, and runs in the other direction.

"At least this thing is still good for something," I say, panting.

Then we run right into penitents.

"Go, go, go!" I quickly tie the tangled mass of

thread around my arm so we don't trip on it as we run through the maze, chased by dead people. A lot of them are old and easy to outrun, but the ones who aren't are generally bigger, stronger, and faster than us. To evade them, we weave in and out of the maze. When we run into a dead end, my already racing heart starts to gallop at breakneck speed. But Kevin just picks up the Staff and beats it against the painted wall. The wall crumbles to smithereens, and we simply run through it.

We nearly run straight into the jaws of an enormous tiger—or at least, more or less a tiger. When it lifts its head and roars, I see that its face is all jaws and hook-like teeth. But Kevin swings the Staff again. *CLANG!* The tooth-faced tiger whimpers and goes racing in the other direction, toward a dead man who immediately starts screaming and running in the *other* other direction.

As we keep running through the Eighth Court, we encounter, and swiftly shoo away with the Staff, all kinds of strange beasts. Some are nasty but basically normal animals, like wasps and scorpions, but others are even worse: vicious dogs with too many teeth, bears with too many mouths, and those horrifying giant murder hornets . . . but with teeth. But they all turn and flee the moment Kevin rings Mùlián's Staff.

The penitents aren't so lucky. While we flee the dead people, the dead people in turn get chased by clouds of killer wasps and flaming bulls and snakes made of scorching hot metal. A penitent corners us down a dead end. But without missing a beat, Kevin smashes through it—to reveal a centipede the size of a Komodo dragon with a wriggling jet-black body, a fire-engine-red head with antennae the size of my forearm, and a hundred human arms that it uses to walk, or crawl, on human-like hands toward us.

When Kevin rings the Staff of Mùlián—*CLANG!*—its disgusting red antennae curl up like it's clenching a fist. Kevin and I slam our backs against the wall as the nightmarish creature barrels past us on its hundred hands and falls lunging upon the penitent. An ear-piercing *CLICK!* of pincers drowns out his screams, and we jump over the smashed remains of the dead end and back out into the maze.

"Hey, why don't you just keep doing that?" I say, pointing at the Staff.

Kevin furrows his brow. "You mean just keep smashing down the walls?"

"Yeah. It'd be faster running through a straight line, right? And since the animals can get the dead people but not us, it'll give them an open line of sight to attack them, too."

Kevin turns to the wall on our right and knocks it over with the Staff. He then slams the next one, then the next, sending them toppling down like dominoes and creating a clear path for us to run.

"Mom?" I shout as we run straight through the collapsed walls. "Mom!"

I tell the spool, "Take us *through* the Eighth Court." We follow the unwinding thread in a diagonal slash all the way across the maze. But even after all that, Mom isn't in this Court, either.

EIGHTEEN

ALONE

The spool has come to a stop, indicating that we've gone through the entire Eighth Court. Still no sign of Mom, and there are only two Courts left.

Did Mom really go all the way, or nearly all the way, into Dìyù? If she was hoping someone from the Guilds could come find her, wouldn't it make it easier for them if she'd just stayed put in one of the earlier Courts?

Against my will, I think again about Dad and then Auntie Kathie, saying Mom's body had been found. I quickly shove it out of my mind—I can't let Dìyù's tricks get to me. Mom has been here for a week and a half, and she doesn't have the Staff of Mùlián to protect her. Who knows why she had to keep moving.

Even though it hurts each time I have to do this *again*, I tell the spool, "Take us to the Ninth Court." It dutifully starts rolling.

I take a step to go, but Kevin stays. He blinks furiously, looking dazed.

"Hey, are you okay?" I ask, suddenly alarmed.

"What? Oh, yeah." Kevin rubs his head again. "Yeah, my head just hurts a little bit from being tackled earlier. But it's not too bad, really. Just hurts a bit."

It takes me a moment to realize he's talking about Wendell Milhaven knocking him to the floor after Yama first made his offer. Has he been like this since the *Fifth Court*? He's seemed okay, but he suddenly looks like he might have had a concussion.

That can be really serious.

Kevin sees me staring and smiles. He smiles a lot, so I might be overreacting, but all I can think about is my dad. "I'm fine. I'm not fated to die here, remember?"

He taps his ankle. That does make me feel better, but *not dying* is a really low bar to clear. He could still get hurt, even badly hurt, and I don't want that to happen, either.

"Right," I say, a sinking feeling in my chest. The terrible truth is, whatever I told him earlier, I'm not worried enough to send him back to Auntie Kathie's apartment if that could jeopardize my chance to find Mom with only two Courts to go. I swallow, then keep going.

The spool leads us toward another staff elevator, camouflaged by a mural of giant tortoises eating people (presumably very slowly). But before we can step inside, a familiar blood-curdling, horribly ravaged voice comes over the intercom.

"INTRUDERS!" King Yama—oh, sorry, Director of the Department of Infernal Affairs—rasps. "I had my officials search our files, and we have located your parent."

My heart somersaults into my throat. They found Mom!

But then Yama continues, "They are still looking for Dawn Liu Huang's file, but we *did* locate the father of one Kevin Brynjar Chengsson, Cheng Wang."

"Hey, that's my dad!" Kevin blurts out, his eyes wide. "Wait, he's in Dìyù, too? Even after all this time?"

I bite my tongue to stop myself from yelling, *Are you KIDDING me?* Which would be kind of insensitive since Kevin just found out his dad has also been in Dìyù this whole time, and he got there the usual way. But I can't believe this. They found *Kevin*'s parent? Really? We didn't even tell them his name! (Which would seem to be Cheng . . . Chengsson?)

"For the last ten years since his untimely murder, Cheng has been in the Court of the Wrongful Dead, watching his widow, Alicia Gangsdottir, hunt down his killers on an infinite loop. Considering there were twelve assassins involved and an entire secret society that hired them, he has a lot of resentment to purge before he can be safely reincarnated," Yama explains.

Kevin exhales, but his relief that his dad hasn't spent all that time in the torture part of Dìyù is short lived.

Yama goes on, "If the intruders do not turn themselves in, he will be removed from the Fourth Court and thrown out into the rest of Dìyù to be tortured with all the other pitiful souls trapped here. *All* the Courts, including the ones whose punishments he hasn't earned from his own misdeeds."

"*What?!*" Kevin shouts. "You—you can't do that!"

"And if you're thinking about filing a complaint, yes, we can do that," Yama says. "Because this is Dìyù, and if you think that's unfair, you should see Heaven." Yama sneers. "And we *will* do that. Unless you're a good son and turn yourself in."

On that sinister—and super condescending—note, the intercom goes silent.

Kevin runs a hand through his hair, clearly in shock. I can't blame him. Even though he said he doesn't have any of his own memories of his dad, he's still his dad. My stomach twists as the cruelty of this dilemma sinks in. Giving up on finding Mom is absolutely not an option. I won't even consider it. But I can't demand Kevin leave *his* parent to just rot in Dìyù.

I break the silence first. "I'm *not* going to turn myself in," I say, my jaw tight.

"I wasn't going to ask you to," Kevin says, though I can see the distress in his eyes.

". . . but I understand that you have to," I finish, even though it makes me feel sick to my stomach. Even though I told him he could go earlier, let's face it, it was easy for me to say that because deep down, I already kind of knew he'd refuse. I know that now.

Kevin blinks. "Really?"

I nod. Swallowing, I press the up button for the elevator. "Take the elevator back up to the Fifth Court and turn yourself in. After you go, I'll go down to the Ninth Court."

Suddenly, I think about Mom's coin flip trick again. I'd insisted that Kevin could just leave me here to find Mom alone, and part of me even wants him to, so I don't have to carry the guilt if something happens to him. But now that he has to leave, I realize how bogus I was, because having to be on my own in Dìyù absolutely terrifies me.

Kevin hesitates, then hands me Mùlián's Staff. He steps into the elevator and holds out his finger to push the button for the fifth floor. But one, two, three seconds pass and he doesn't press. "Hey, do you know what Fire Elder told me before we left?"

I remember the head of the Warriors' parting words to Kevin: *Remember what I told you.*

"No. What?" I'm guessing it wasn't to believe in himself. Fire Elder didn't seem like that kind of guy.

"So the Guilds is short for the 'Gold Mountain Guilds,' right? That's because Gold Mountain is what the very first Chinese immigrants to America called California. Anyway, basically Fire Elder was saying that the Guilds talk a lot about preserving thousands of years of tradition and stuff, but we're the descendants of the people who left."

"That's kind of a mean thing to say."

Kevin shrugs. "Knowing Fire Elder, I don't think he's saying it like it's a bad thing. After he told me that, he said it's really brave and honorable of you to go, but honor is for suckers. It doesn't win battles, and you have to know when to retreat."

Cyrus Lie: definitely not a "believe in yourself" kind of guy.

"I know you don't wanna give up on your mom, and I think that's awesome," Kevin says. "But I don't wanna never see you again, either. If it gets really dangerous in the last two Courts, or the penitents try to 'turn you off and turn you back on' again . . . please go back home through the painting, okay? I know I said I didn't know your mom that well, but I know she'd want you to."

I think about helping Mom set up our hot pot for Thanksgiving and Christmas and New Year's Eve dinners—I have to help her, because Dad is too handsome to do it. I think about singing along to Disney songs on the way to Las Vegas to keep Mona Li entertained. I even remember that dark time at the beginning of sixth grade, when Mom downloaded some mindfulness app and made me wake up early to do guided meditations with her every weekend. I was so frustrated about it because she *sucks* at meditation—and if you think it's not possible to be bad at meditation, you've never seen my mom try to just sit still and relax. But now I realize she was just trying to bond with me.

"Okay."

Kevin's shoulders relax, and he presses the button. He's still waving at me until the door is fully closed and I can't see him anymore. Heck, for all I know he could still be waving.

I clench my fists and tap my foot as the elevator goes up, up, up, up to the Fifth Court. When I press the button again and the doors swing open, the elevator is empty. I step inside and press the second-to-last *4* button from the bottom. But as the doors start to close, I lean forward and hold the button to open them.

I look out at the Eighth Court for a moment. Out at the uncertain tortures ahead, feeling less ready than ever. One last deep breath.

Then I unzip the purse and toss Wood Elder's painting of Auntie Kathie's apartment out before releasing the open-doors button and riding alone down to the Ninth Court.

Auntie Kathie would lose her mind at what I just did. Thida would tell me it's really, really stupid. And I'm sure Mom would be disappointed in me for making a promise just to break it. But she'll have to tell me how disappointed she is to my face, because I'm not leaving Dìyù without her.

In the short time it takes for the elevator to go down one story to the Ninth Court, I already start to regret throwing the painting away.

Imaginary Auntie Kathie and Thida aren't wrong, but what I just did wasn't *completely* thoughtless. My thinking was, once I've found Mom and she's clearly still alive, we can just turn ourselves in like Kevin and be escorted out. Heck, maybe we'll let one of the penitents turn us in, preferably someone who doesn't have a racist tattoo or a "very popular" true crime program about them. Getting rid of the painting was just getting rid of the temptation to teleport out of Dìyù once things got scary, which I wouldn't be able to take back and would regret for the rest of my life.

But okay, it was definitely a reckless thing to do.

I guess I'll have to find her, then. It's not like I have a choice anymore.

The elevator doors open, and I step out into the Ninth Court. Even though there are only two Courts left where she could be, after entering a new Court and failing to find Mom eight different times now, it hurts—it *physically* hurts—to get my hopes up and have them crushed again and again each time.

Then I step out of the elevator and see her.

"Mom?" I say, my throat tight. For a second, I don't believe it. But she's standing in the middle of the dark hallway, her hands in the pockets of her hand-sewn violet collared shirt and matching pencil skirt, smelling of banana milk and looking like a Chinese American Peggy Carter. She looks unsurprised to see me, as if she's been expecting me. But then her mouth falls open, revealing her slightly crooked teeth.

"Evie," she murmurs, holding her arms out toward me.

"Mom!" I drop the Staff of Mùlián as I run forward to embrace her, overwhelmed with emotion as the tears burn in my eyes.

But less than half a second after I fling my arms around her, I draw back, gasping with pain.

Mom is gone. Standing in her place is a free-standing brass pillar, glowing red hot as if a fire is heating it on the inside. Even though I only hugged it for an instant before pulling away, the sleeves of my stolen sweatshirt have been burned straight through. But the pain from embracing the scorching hot metal is still nothing compared to the crushing disappointment of realizing it wasn't Mom.

"Evie Mei?" A shadow appears at the end of the hall, and I tear my eyes up from the spot on the floor where I really thought my mom had been standing just moments before.

"Evie!" Mom (?) says. "Oh, Evie, I knew you could do it."

Even though my arms are still stinging from the pillar, I have to stop myself from running forward to hug her again. Swallowing, I pick up the Staff of Mùlián and ring it tentatively.

CLANG! In an instant, "Mom" fades away, once again revealing a superheated brass pillar.

My heart pounding, I run through the halls, shouting, "Mom?" and ringing the Staff. But again and again Mom appears, and again and again I ring the Staff and she's revealed to be a scorching hot pillar. Soon my eyes are stinging worse than the faint burn mark on my arms.

"MOM!" I shout, my voice cracking with desperation.

Again, I hear her high-pitched, almost girlish voice saying, "Evie!" And yet again I wave the Staff and reveal her to just be an illusion.

I don't realize how badly I'm shaking until my knees knock together and I nearly topple over. I had managed to suck it up and keep going each time I left a Court without Mom, and when we were getting bombarded by mobs of dead people, and even when I saw Dad and Auntie Kathie saying that Mom's body had been found and this whole search was just a cruel trick of infernally unfair proportions. But now, standing in the second-to-last Court of Dìyù, surrounded by illusions of my mom that will sear the skin off my arms if I try to hug her, I lose it.

Screaming, I fling the Staff to the ground and bury my face in my hands. Once again, I remind myself that Mom is waiting for me, that I don't have time to wallow, so even though this is the *tenth time* I've done this now, my trembling fingers tug on the spool, which is sitting on the ground at my feet.

"Take me to the—" I begin, but my voice is so choked up, I can barely get the words out.

I look at the spool. By now, the red thread is completely untangled. When I look up again, I'm surrounded by a circle of Moms, all looking identical and alive and perfect. I want to believe with all my heart that one *must* be the real Mom, that I can't have gone through nine out of the Ten Courts of Dìyù just for an illusion. But I know it doesn't work like that, and if I try to hug all of them, I'll just burn myself.

"One Court left," I try to tell myself, but my voice falters. Instead, other voices echo in my mind:

I can still identify her from her clothes. I'd know Dawn's work anywhere.

You're not under my jurisdiction, so I couldn't technically punish you even if I wanted to.

Th-they just found her body.

"Evie?" all the Moms say in unison. But when I swing the Staff, they're all swept away to reveal glowing brass pillars. With the Ninth Court suddenly silent, I can hear how heavily I'm breathing. I shudder, then sink to my feet, hugging my knees.

Mom isn't in the Ninth Court, and I won't find her in the Tenth Court, either.

What I saw in the Seventh Court was no illusion. My mom really *is* dead.

NINETEEN
CONFESSION

Until now, I hadn't realized just how *tired* I am. Since entering Dìyù, I've always been on the move. But now that I can actually take a moment to catch my breath—now that I know it didn't matter how fast I got through the other Courts—all the built-up exhaustion of the day hits me at once like a tidal wave. I can barely stand.

So I just sit and let it wash over me. I hadn't realized I'd dropped the spool until I see the handkerchief—which is physically attached to it since I couldn't cut the thread to sew the letters with—lying on the ground next to my messed-up sneakers. New hot-pink words have formed. Auntie Kathie's needle-writing is now messy and cursive, like she was sewing as fast and furiously as she could. But her message is clear: *FOUND YOUR MOM'S BODY PLS COME HOME.*

Mom is dead. And since Monk never had any idea where she was, she was probably dead the whole time. Before we even stepped foot in Dìyù.

Would it still be possible to get her out of Dìyù if she's dead? I look at the Staff of Mùlián, remembering that its original owner set out to rescue *his* mom from Dìyù. And now I'm pretty sure I know where she is. She can't still be in the First Court awaiting judgment, because the spool didn't start tangling until the Third Court. As a . . . as a dead person she has no reason to be in the Fifth Court, and I've just searched the Sixth through Ninth Courts. I guess she could be in the final Court, but given how slowly things move down here, it seems really unlikely. More likely she's in the one Court we didn't search all the way: the Fourth Court, the Court of the Wrongful Dead.

I'm already here, aren't I? I can still try. I don't have to retreat just yet. And if she really is in the Court of the Wrongful Dead, that would mean her death wasn't an accident at all. Someone is responsible. Even if I can't bring her back, I have to find out who.

Taking a deep breath, I get to my feet. But as I'm walking back toward the elevator, a blur in white sweats emerges from behind a brass pillar and charges at me. Before I have time to react, the penitent has scooped up the spool, still tied to my little finger, and yanks me toward him.

"Hey! Let go!" I swing the Staff of Mùlián at my attacker, a disheveled-looking man with a lumpy, unshaven face, only for him to knock it out of my hand. He continues to pull on the thread, and though I try to resist, he's bigger and stronger than me and pulls me in easily. I hurry to untie the thread from my pinkie and run, but nearly collide into a scorching hot brass pillar and stop in my tracks.

"I saw you before, but thought you were just another pillar. Until you used this." Lumpy-Face holds up the Staff, revealing callused white burn marks across his palms. At first I thought he was just really ugly, but now I realize that his face is swollen up all over, like he was stung by dozens of angry bees . . . or murder hornets. It's hard to read his face, but the corner of his mouth curves up into the faintest hint of a smile.

"I'm not an evil man. I don't want to hurt you. I just want to get out of this place," he says. "But I'm not a good one, either, so I will if you try and stop me. Do I make myself clear?"

He cocks his head as he waits for the message to sink in. He's just as desperate as I am and also twice my size. Kevin and I have managed to escape capture by way more people through a combination of resourcefulness and luck, not to mention various magical objects. But now I'm alone and defenseless. And anyway, Mom is dead. She was dead this whole time. It really would make a lot of sense to just turn myself in and bring an end to this nightmare—at least, the one in Dìyù. The real nightmare started ten days ago, when Mom died.

At the same time, I still can't abandon my quest to find her now that I know where she is. I think again about her coin-flip trick, and how once the coin had landed, she knew what she really wanted.

"Okay. I'll go with you," I say. "But"—I turn and point toward where the elevator is hidden—"it'd be faster if we went that way."

If I thought trudging through the dark, winding passageways of Dìyù with Kevin was awkward before, it's nothing compared to taking an elevator ride back up to the Fifth Court with this strange man, who for all I know might be a murderer.

"So you came to see your mom, huh?" Lumpy-Face says as the elevator goes up.

I stare at him in shock. "H-how did you—" I stammer, before remembering that Yama revealed as much in his most recent message over the intercom. "Yeah," I say flatly.

It hits me again that she's really dead. *Again.*

A moment of awkward silence passes. Then Lumpy-Face says, "I'm sorry to hear that."

This never really seems to get less awkward. "Thanks," I say stiffly, folding my arms across my chest. "I'm, uh, I'm sorry you died, too." It's hard to tell exactly how old Lumpy-Face is with his swollen face. His hair is starting to gray, so he probably wasn't that young when he died. But only starting, so I would guess he wasn't old, either.

"It's all good. Just sorry I ended up down here, though I can't say it was a surprise, if I'm being honest."

"Hmm."

I continue staring at the wall, but then Lumpy-Face says, "So was it recent, or . . . ?"

Are we really having this conversation? "Yeah. Ten

days ago." I think—I realize with a sinking feeling that I don't know for sure. Did she die when she went missing and they only just found her body, or . . .

Lumpy-Face clicks his tongue. "I'm sorry."

"You know, it's my birthday, too."

"Aw, really? I'm sorry. Happy birthday."

This conversation is so bizarre that I can't help but laugh, but it's a sad, bitter one. Everything I've been through to find Mom, and now I'm in an elevator getting more meaningless condolences (and birthday wishes), from some random dead guy.

"What is it, eleven? Twelve?"

I don't answer—I guess it's a normal question to ask about someone's birthday, but I'm a little wary about this stranger trying to chat with me about this.

But then Lumpy-Face muses, "Coming down here—I guess you loved her a lot, huh?"

I remember Mona Li slamming the door in my face this afternoon. It makes me dizzy to think that was today, it seems so long ago, but I can hear her words as clearly as if she's yelling them at me right now. *You complained about Mom to Thida all the time before, so don't act like you're sad now.*

When I don't respond, Lumpy-Face raises an eyebrow. So far, I'd avoided looking at him too closely because, well—and I'm not saying this to be mean—his face is really gross and hard to look at. Glancing at him now, I notice that most of his eyebrow seems to have been singed off—was it from grabbing a brass pillar? "More complicated than that?"

"No, I loved her." So, so much. "But . . ." My hand has reached for the red string necklace my mom made to protect me, and I run it through my fingers like Āh Mā does with her prayer beads as I continue. For reasons I can't explain, I suddenly feel an urge to tell this complete stranger the secret weight that I've been carrying around in my heart. It's not Mona Li's fault that it's there. My sister just had the guts to say out loud what I had been secretly thinking. "But sometimes, I feel like I don't even have the right to say that. Because when she . . . when she was alive, I wasted so much time focusing on what I didn't like about her."

My voice cracks, and I squeeze the string harder.

"Hmm." Lumpy-Face scratches his swelled-up temple. "I know my opinion probably isn't good for much, but it seems to me that you didn't love your mom any less just because you complained about her sometimes. It seems to me that's just being a child."

"It was more than sometimes," I blurt out, *a lot more.*

But he continues, "You can love your mom even if you knew she had her flaws. In fact, the way I see it, that's the only way you can really love anybody."

I think about this for a while, then stare at him, speechless. Somehow, that's the most helpful thing an adult has told me since she died, and it's from a random guy in Dìyù. He might not be a murderer or the kind of person who would tattoo RACIST on his face for the whole world to see, but by his own admission he wasn't a good man.

But going by his logic, even if he clearly has done some things he regrets, that doesn't have to mean he can't give some good advice, too.

"Th-thanks," I say finally. He just nods, and I think, whatever else this guy had done in his most recent life, there'll always be one person out there grateful to him for this.

When I look at the wall again, I see that the button for the seventh floor has lit up. Lumpy-Face lets out a low whistle and raps the Staff of Mùlián against the wall, then winces as it *CLANG*s. My eyes dart from him to the door. If I time it right, can I grab the Staff and run just as it opens?

"So this thing is magic, huh?" he says, peering at the Staff. "The way the big guy was talking, I was expecting it to shoot fireballs or some such." He clicks his tongue again.

"Oh. Yeah, it belonged to a monk a long time ago. I think it can damage anything or anyone that's from Dìyù, like the buildings and the employees. But it doesn't work on the dead souls who were sent down here, which is why Yama had to send you guys after us."

I inch closer to the buttons, getting ready to "accidentally" press the next one. Maybe the sudden stop will take him by surprise long enough for me to grab the Staff and then find another way up to the Fourth Court.

But Lumpy-Face abruptly turns his lumpy face toward me.

"So, this right here is how you broke into Dìyù?" he says. "And it can get past security?"

In an instant, I realize what I've done. But it's already too late. Without warning, he turns the Staff and bangs it against the elevator door like it's a battering ram. *CLANG!* The elevator smashes open.

"No!" I lunge toward him, but he's already sprinted off through the gaping hole where the doors used to be, like he's the Road Runner running through a brick wall in the Wile E. Coyote cartoons.

"Hey! Get back here with that!" I shout. "I need that to save—"

But then the elevator starts moving again, and I fall backward against the remaining wall to keep myself from falling out the open doors. I crawl toward the wall as the elevator takes me up without the Staff of Mùlián.

TWENTY
REUNION

I look at the giant hole in the elevator doors, furious with myself for revealing the Staff's power to Lumpy-Face. But I couldn't have known it would matter to him, because he already had me as his get-out-of-Dìyù-free card. Why would he need to escape with the Staff when all he had to do was turn me in to Yama?

But I have bigger questions to worry about, like how I'm supposed to get Mom out now without the Staff.

If Mom weren't really dead, then all I'd have to do is find her and then turn ourselves in so Yama could send us both home. But she *is* dead, and there's no way he'll just let me leave with her now. I could have tried to see if she could teleport back to Earth through the painting of Auntie Kathie's apartment, except I threw it away.

How could I have screwed up this badly?

The elevator stops in the Fifth Court; I look out through the hole at the office buildings. Kevin is somewhere there, turning himself in. Is it time for me to do the same? To retreat?

But as I look out the elevator, I remember tossing the painting out before descending to the Ninth Court. If it's still in front of the elevator in the Eighth Court, I just have to press a button and can retrieve it within seconds.

I press the third-to-last *4* button for eight (still hasn't gotten less annoying). Because of the hole in the elevator door, I can see even before arriving in the Eighth Court that the painting is right where I left it.

But as the elevator gets closer before coming to a stop, I see that the delicate paper is in several pieces, dirty hoof and claw tracks all over Wood Elder's work.

For a moment I just stand there, staring at the shredded remains of the painting. I've never wished I could punch myself in the face before, but if there's a first time for everything, it makes sense it would be on this terrible day. Who did I think I am, calling *Mom* arrogant? Now I have no allies, no Staff of Mùlián to scare away demons, and no way to get Mom home.

And yet, I *still* can't bring myself to just turn myself in and leave Mom behind. I've come all this way, and even if she was really dead this whole time, she's *here*. She's *close*—I know she is. The spool said so. Maybe I can't bring her back to the living, but while I'm here, I can at least see her again.

Auntie Kathie, Thida, and at this point, even Kevin would tell me not to put myself in any more danger now that I've lost the Staff. But if she is in the Court of the Wrongful Dead, that really isn't that scary. And now that I think about it, losing the Staff might make it *easier* for me to find Mom, because now I look just like the penitents.

The more I think about it, I realize there's still hope. I lost the Staff and threw away the painting, but I still have the handkerchief. I can needle-text Auntie Kathie to have Wood Elder make another one on joss paper and burn it. Then Mom and I can teleport back home.

I press the fourth *4* button—the Fourth Court. The elevator moves back up, and my heart skips a beat when I see penitents wandering the halls. But when I step out into the hallway, they run straight past me. Like I suspected, now that I'm dressed like everybody else and not carrying the Staff of Mùlián anymore, they can't tell just by looking at me that I'm the intruder.

I glance around the Court of the Wrongful Dead, with its endless halls of numbered doors.

One at a time, I think as I reach for the nearest door. But then I hesitate.

What if the dead people in the Court of the Wrongful Dead try to turn me in, too? They might not be as desperate to get out of here as the other inhabitants of Dìyù, but this is just a temporary situation: Eventually, they'll have to do their time in the rest of Dìyù like everyone else. And thanks to Yama announcing he'd taken Kevin's dad as a hostage not too long ago, everyone here will remember that. If I reveal myself to someone else, they'll probably try and turn me in, too. But how else am I supposed to find which room Mom is in?

I pinch the red string pendant between my fingernails. Suddenly I feel a surge of anger: My mother's protection spell hadn't been able to keep the worst from happening to our family, so what good was it even for? But then I think about all the close calls I'd had in Dìyù: how I'd suddenly become calm while sinking in the pool of blood, the string staying secure in the Sixth Court even with loads of dead people climbing it. I'd been too petty to admit that I'd actually gotten a *lot* of help from the Guilds, but Earth Elder had given me a magic item, too.

Suddenly I remember asking Auntie Kathie if the string around my neck would be able to point me to Mom, since she'd enchanted it for me. Auntie Kathie had said probably—she just didn't want me to do it because she didn't want me to undo the protection charm. Maybe she's right, but I'm not dangling over swords or running from angry animals on fire in this Court. I just need to find one door.

Acting quickly, I untie the red string pendant from my neck and tie it around the spool. "Take me to Mom," I say, then release it. The spool rolls down the hallway, and I chase after it. It doesn't tangle, and my heart catches in my throat . . .

. . . and then suddenly, it jerks left, coming to a stop in front of Room #51960.

For a moment, I just stand there, staring in disbelief at the straight red line between me and the door. But then I run forward and grab the handle, my heart pounding. The door is locked and I can't just smash it down anymore, so I knock. "Hello?"

I keep banging until suddenly the door swings open, and my heart stops. Because at long last, there she is, standing right in front of me.

"Mom?"

For real this time.

"Evie!" Her mouth falls open. "Why are you he—"

Her voice goes up an octave, like it always does when she's heated, or seized with emotion. Remembering that I'm still Dìyù's Most Wanted, I clamp my hand over her mouth in case there's anyone around who might hear. She pulls me into the room and I push the door shut behind me, but at least one person already overheard.

"Hey, keep it down!" someone yells. Strangely, there's no video playing in this room, so we can hear the murder victim next door banging furiously on the wall. "Some of us are trying to watch! Were you raised by wolves?"

"Does your butt hurt from sitting up on your high horse?" Mom shouts back, and I almost tear up because I've missed this annoying, difficult, awesome woman so much.

Mom is dressed in the same shapeless white

clothes as the inhabitants of Dìyù. This might be the first time I've ever seen Mom in clothes she didn't make herself; I'm sure if I asked, she would have a lot to say about the subpar craftsmanship. But that's not the only thing jarring about Mom's outfit. Even though I'd already suspected it, it still feels like a gut punch to have it confirmed: Mom really is dead.

Mom turns from the wall back toward me. Her brown eyes are filled with horror, and I remember that I'm also dressed like a penitent, not to mention the dried blood still covering my face.

"I'm not dead," I say quickly. Mom exhales in relief, but she doesn't ask me if I'm the intruder. I guess somehow, she didn't hear Yama's announcement—maybe because she was engrossed in watching whoever wronged her die.

So I explain the whole story. I start with how I found Monk in the shop and his fake story about taking her to Dìyù—even though Mom is standing in front of me, it still hurts to recount how I fell for the lie—and then how I found the Guilds, and how they gave me the Staff of Mùlián.

"So, let me get this straight," Mom interrupts. For once, I'm not annoyed by it. She must have a *lot* of questions. "You went to the Guilds for help, and they let you come to Dìyù *by yourself*?"

"I didn't come here by myself. This one kid from the Warriors, Kevin Chengsson, came with me."

"Kevin Cheng—" Mom's jaw drops. "Alicia's kid? *That's* who Fire Elder sent with you to *Dìyù*?" She groans. "Do I want to know what happened to him?"

I feel the urge to defend Kevin, but decide that's not really the most important thing right now. "And then, uh, a lot of other things happened after that," I continue, which is putting it mildly. "But now I'm here, and we have to figure out how to get you out of Dìyù." I show her the handkerchief with my lackluster but magical embroidery. Breathlessly I explain to her my plan, how I can needle-write because she taught me, how I can ask Auntie Kathie for another painting . . .

But Mom's face is grave. "Oh, Evie," she says softly when I finish. "I can't landscape travel out of Dìyù."

I feel like I had the power to fly, but then somehow lost it midair. After I'd already gotten about a hundred feet off the ground.

"Okay," I say, trying to stay calm. "Well, there has to be another way. Some Weaver spell or something . . . right?" My voice comes out so small, it could fit through the eye of a needle as I repeat, "Right?"

"No, it's not that," Mom says, right before she confirms my worst fear. "I can't leave Dìyù at all. Because . . ."

Because she's dead. Of course she can't. I'd feared as much already, ever since the Ninth—no, the Seventh Court. But I hadn't really believed it could be true. I can't have come all this way and finally *have found Mom*, only for her to be stuck here for good, or for however long she's supposed to be stuck here.

"But . . . but Mùlián saved *his* mom from Dìyù."

"He actually didn't," Mom says. "Mùlián was able to infiltrate Dìyù with the Staff, but he couldn't take his mother back with him. There's no way to take someone who's dead from Dìyù before they've done their time. He had to rescue his mother's soul 'through devotion,' and who knows if that part's true. He was a monk; of course he would say that."

Dad always says that I got my sarcasm from Mom. "But . . ." I know how small I sound, like I'm a little kid pleading to stay up just a little longer before bedtime. "But can't we just try? What do we have to lose, right?"

Mom reaches out and moves a flyaway strand of hair behind my ear, like she's done a million times. I don't push her hand away in annoyance like I usually do, though. "It doesn't—it doesn't always work like that, Evie."

"But why not? I'm already here, aren't I? I came all this way." Mom bites down on her lower lip, and for the first time I become aware that she's fighting back tears. I know it's not her that I'm angry at, and I know it's not fair to put her through this, but . . . "I don't understand."

Her arms are around me, enveloping me in the scent of her favorite banana milk body lotion. This is what kept me going all this time, the thought of embracing my mom after finding her again in Dìyù. Only it isn't triumphant like I imagined it would be. It's a pity hug.

But then she kisses my forehead, and I feel a jolt: Her flesh is cold to the touch. And then I remember that Mom's body was found, and because ten days have passed, it doesn't even look like her anymore. I remember that awful demon woman in the Fifth Court saying that Li Jianyu has nothing to return to.

All of a sudden, I do understand. That doesn't mean I like it, or that I ever will. It doesn't mean there's a reason, good or bad, that somehow makes my mom's death okay or fair. But I do understand that she's gone, and she can't come back.

Mom holds me for a while, until I summon the strength to ask. "We thought it was an accident, but the Court of the Wrongful Dead is for people who were murdered." I swallow. "Who killed you? Does it have to do with the Spindle of Fate?"

Mom's face had been a tapestry of interwoven emotions—sympathy, resignation, an unbearable sorrow that mirrors my own—but suddenly her upper lip curls up. Her eyes, which had been so soft and loving only moments before, suddenly spark with fury. "It was The Gambler."

"Auntie Kathie's ex?" I blurt out, completely blindsided by this answer. "But why?"

"He found out about the Spindle. I can't be sure, but I wouldn't be surprised if he wooed your auntie to get to it." If I'd thought my mom's voice was dripping with venom whenever she talked about my aunt's loser ex before, I had no idea. "He tried to use your aunt's pregnancy to get me to change his fate. I told him I'd sooner eat the Spindle than use it to help a lowlife like him. If you gave this guy a million dollars, he'd blow it all betting on the National Spelling Bee."

She shakes her head. "He's got a sense of humor, I'll give him that. When I woke up, I was in the ocean with a rope around my hands and the Spindle of

Fate stuffed inside my mouth. Since it was made in Heaven, it's impossibly dense, so—"

So she sank. Mom recounts her own death matter-of-factly—I think she's trying to be strong for me, but it just makes what she's describing even more upsetting somehow. But she can't hide the bitterness in her voice as she describes this horrible irony: how the Spindle, the source of her power and our family's legacy, was used to bring about her death. As cruel as that is, I'm even more upset to learn that Mom really *did* drown. I'd hoped that if she had been murdered, maybe it could at least have been a quick and relatively painless way.

Mom walks over toward the bed. Perfectly made, because of course my mom is still making her bed even when her life is over. A wooden object sits next to where a pillow would normally be, and I feel a jolt when I realize what it is: a spindle, the wisp of a new thread around it. Even though it must be hundreds, if not thousands, of years old, the spindle doesn't look much different from any of the others lying around the tailor shop. But the thread seems to draw all the light in the room toward it, even though it doesn't look like it's made of gold or silver or anything else shiny.

"So that's the Spindle of Fate," I mutter. I guess I could show more respect, but I can barely bring myself to feel any awe or wonder or any other positive feelings toward the family heirloom. Not when it killed my mom: not just by bringing The Gambler into our lives, but it *literally* killed her.

"Since it was inside my mouth when I died, I guess it came with me. Or maybe an illusion of it." Mom picks up the Spindle, caressing it gently as she turns it over in her slender Weaver's fingers. I guess she has no hard feelings, and I can't say she should—her beloved dad gave it to her, and his ancestors gave it to him before that. But looking at it makes me feel sick.

"You said Auntie Kathie explained how it works to you?" she said softly. "As much as she could, anyway."

I'm not sure why she wants to talk about this now, but I nod. "Yeah, she said it can weave threads of fate. Which basically can change a person's destiny, but you can't control how."

Mom nods. "More or less." She looks up from the Spindle and back at me. "Evie, listen carefully. There's something I need you to do for me."

"What is it?"

"I've seen The Gambler's fate here." Mom points at the projector screen behind us. I was too focused on my mom to notice before, but now I see that it's paused on a blurry freeze-frame of a man with his back turned to the "camera," or however Dìyù gets this footage of people's fates. "When your Auntie Kathie finds out that he killed me, she becomes so angry that she kills him."

Mom sighs, like she always does when she's talking about her little sister's impulsive decisions. But all I can think is *Good for her*.

"I'm going to teach you to use the Spindle of Fate. When you get back home, you need to weave a new thread for him so that this doesn't happen."

It takes a moment for me to understand what my mom's saying. Mom is asking me to change The Gambler's fate . . . which would mean saving his life.

"You—you want me to *save* him?" I say, stunned. "But why?"

"Because I love my family more than I hate him," Mom replies. "And I hated him a *lot*, even before he killed me. But if your aunt gets her revenge the way I've seen her fated to do, she'll go to prison for a long time. And her kid on the way—your cousin—will grow up like an orphan. I can't let that happen."

My mom's firm voice goes up an octave. I know how much she loves her family—I've never doubted it—and I love Auntie Kathie, too, but . . . "I—I can't do that."

"I'll walk you through it step-by-step so you know exactly what to do. As you can see, I've already started it." She looks down at the half-woven wisp of thread. "I thought it was going to be the last thread of fate that our family would ever spin, but now that you're here, you can take the Spindle back and keep our family's most precious tradition alive. However, that does mean it'll have to fall on you to finish what I've started."

Mom sets the Spindle in my hand. Her touch is cold, but that isn't why I recoil.

Boiling with rage, I throw the Spindle across the room.

"*No,*" I say firmly. Mom's mouth falls open, exposing her crooked teeth. "I won't do it. I came all this way—I *literally went through Hell* because I thought I was going to save *you*. Not the person who *killed you.*"

"Don't yell at me, Evie," Mom says, but I'm too upset to listen.

"You always told me I could succeed as long as I worked hard. You lied to me!" It's a childish thing to say, and I know it. But I've tried *so hard* to be mature, to grit my teeth and grow up for my family's sake, and look what that's gotten me. I even somehow found a way to keep it together when I found out that this entire horrible quest was just a lie, that Mom was dead all along. But this—*this* is too much.

"I won't do it! I won't. It's not—"

My voice cracks, and suddenly it's like all the tears I hadn't cried before—not at the funeral, not when I was being chased all over Dìyù, not even when I realized for the second time that my mom was dead—come out all at once. "It's not fair," I sob. "It's *not fair.*"

"I know," Mom says. She holds me as I break down crying in her arms. "I know, honey, I know."

TWENTY-ONE
CONSOLATION

Mom doesn't bring up the Spindle of Fate again, but she doesn't have to. I'm still not happy about it, but I don't want to waste any of the precious time I have with her getting into a fight. And I understand she has to protect her sister to the end. I can't understand how she can let her own murder go, but my mom was completely right about one thing: She truly, deeply loves her family.

So as painful as it is, I reluctantly agree to finish what she started. Which means I also have to agree not to tell Auntie Kathie that the father of her baby killed her beloved sister—at least, not until I've finished weaving The Gambler's new thread of fate. I'm even less thrilled about Mom's insistence that I "am not, under any circumstances, to pursue vengeance against that man" myself. She makes it very clear that

I am to complete her existing thread of fate so that "Kathie *does not* kill him in a vengeful rage," instead of weaving a thread so he "spontaneously combusts" or "gets diarrhea and then drowns in his own toilet," because I barely know what I'm doing and trying to change a thread once it's started could go horribly wrong.

As Mom teaches me how to weave the thread of fate, I don't fidget or wish I were watching TV like I did all the other times she tried to teach me her craft. Instead, I watch her intently, committing what she's doing to memory. Mostly I want to have a nice final memory with her, but also, even though I have more mixed feelings than ever about the Spindle itself (Mom reminds me that I'll be the head of the Weavers now, but I could truly not care less about that right now), I'm surprised at how eager I am to learn Mom's secret art and to keep it alive. Even if I'd rather she was.

"Usually, it would take years for me to teach you how to weave a proper thread," Mom murmurs with a wistful sigh. Watching her at her work, I think I can guess why she missed Yama's announcements; it wasn't because she was distracted by the screen in the room. When my mom is fully focused on her craft, she concentrates so intensely, she might block out the rest of the world if she weren't here with me. "Since I've already started it, the hard part is over; you just have to keep going. But to learn to weave new threads of your own, you'll have to consult our family book."

"Family book?"

Mom nods. "Learning from a book instead of a teacher is really not the ideal way to learn what we do. But since there could only ever be one teacher at a time, our ancestors wrote the process down in code in case they died before they had passed it down to their children. Of course they wrote in Chinese, but your grandfather translated their writings to coded English. He was aware that someday his descendants might not be able to read Chinese."

Mom purses her lips, and I wonder if the reason she agreed so readily not to send us to Chinese school was because she felt she owed it to my dad for keeping so many secrets from him. I really don't know what to make of my grandpa. He clearly wasn't clinging *that* tightly to tradition, and Auntie Kathie insisted that he really did want to teach my mom, not just because he had no better options. But at the same time, he still made her make that promise.

Mom explains the code to me. "It's what's called a

cipher, meaning all the letters are substituted for different ones. To switch the letters back, you just need to know the keyword. But in this case, it's not a single word but a poem." She picks up the handkerchief, raising an eyebrow at the clumsy makeshift needle, and stitches a short four-line poem into the cloth. Very neatly, even with a hair pin.

"You're probably wondering why I didn't tell you about any of this before. Did your aunt tell you already?"

I nod. I still don't know how I feel about Mom's promise, but I'm not going to fight with her about it. This is the last conversation I'm going to have with my mom. Why ruin it?

"Yeah. She said you promised my grandpa you wouldn't tell Dad, so you couldn't tell me when I was little because I might tell him." That hurt for a while, but if I'm being honest, I definitely would have told him, and not by accident, either. I've never liked adults lying to me, and I would have hated the idea of lying to Dad. "And she said you didn't tell me later because you were going to pass the Spindle of Fate to Mona Li, not me."

That's one thing I don't have to pretend I'm not angry about, at least. I'd even been thinking about teaching Mona Li the secret and letting her have the Spindle to pass down to her future kids, if she has any. It always should have been hers anyway, and I think it would mean a lot to her even if Mom can't be the one to teach her. But I still have to be the one to finish weaving the thread to change The Gambler's fate. As much as it makes me sick, I can't possibly put something like that on my little sister. Not when Mom was her favorite person in the world.

Mom's cold touch still feels like a shard of ice in my heart, but I don't flinch from it anymore as she squeezes my hand.

"I was hoping to start teaching your sister next year. But it wasn't because I thought you weren't good enough." I hadn't asked that, but I guess I was wondering it a little bit, because it feels good to hear her say it. "You've always been so independent. Even when you were still learning to walk, you wouldn't let me hold your hand and help you no matter how many times you fell." Mom laughs at the memory. "You hadn't even learned to ride a bike yet when you told me for the first time that you wanted to decide your own fate. It took me a while to listen, but when I did, I realized I should honor that."

I hadn't expected this answer, but I don't hate it.

And yet, here I am, learning my mother's most precious craft after all, because it'd die with her otherwise. Funny how fate works sometimes.

"If I get married, will I have to keep this a secret, too?" I probably should keep the question to myself, since I might not like the answer. But it's not like that's ever stopped me.

But Mom snorts. "I was ten years old when I made that promise to my bàba. I was so happy to learn to use the Spindle, and so far away from thinking about marriage, I didn't even understand what I was promising. I'm grateful to him, I really am, but I would never ask you to make me the same promise. Not just because it's sexist, but it's so, so lonely." But Mom adds, "But be very careful who you do tell about it. Don't tell anyone that you can't completely trust. Not just with your own life, but your sister's and your father's and your auntie's, too."

I can't argue with that. After all, the entire reason we're here in the netherworld is because the wrong person found out.

"The family book is in the drawer below the altar in the shop with your grandparents' pictures. My plastic pink binder also has a list of everyone I've ever woven a thread for. It's not long, but every person on that list understands that I could call on them for help someday in return. If our family ever has a problem that your father or your aunt can't solve, you go straight to that list."

So Mom really can still protect us even now that she's gone. I guess I don't have to worry anymore about whether the family business can stay afloat without her. "Not that you need to worry about your dad," she adds reassuringly. "Believe me. I could never marry a weak man."

That's *so* Mom—even when she's trying to praise my dad, she can't resist praising herself, too. I almost roll my eyes, but as full of herself as Mom can be, she's not wrong. And it does make me feel a little better about what I saw Dad confess at the Tower of Viewing Home.

Mom undoes and redoes my braid, which at that point had been in shambles with all the running around in Dìyù. It's still coated in dried blood from the Second Court, so it feels silly to be worried about it being messy. But I'm pretty sure my mom would start twisting her own fingers if they sat still for too long, so I let her.

"Just look out for your sister, okay?" she says. Her voice cracks, and she takes a deep breath before continuing, "You and your dad have always been so close, and that's a beautiful thing, but I don't want her to worry she'll be left out."

As much as I'd worried about Mona Li, I hadn't even thought about that. After Mom's fixed my hair, she takes the red string necklace from the spool and reties it into an intricate knotted pendant. When she's finished, she reties it around my neck. She's silent for a while before she says, "You should get going. I don't know what time it is—it all blurs together after a while—but eventually your father's going to worry."

My heart sinks. I know she's right, and I can't just stay here with her forever, as much as I want to. I have my living family to take care of now. So I get up without an argument, but then realize Mom was wrong about one thing. There *is* a way that I can get her out of here.

"Yama promised to reduce the sentences of anyone who could catch us," I explain. "You could turn me in, and once your time in this Court is over, you wouldn't have to spend any more time in Dìyù. You could just go straight ahead to the next life."

If I can't take Mom back home, at least I can make sure that she doesn't have to spend a minute in the other Courts.

Mom's face twitches. "That's very sweet, Evie, but I'm not going to eat from my daughter's leg just because I'm starving."

"I won't really be in trouble, though," I insist. "Yama just wants to get me out of here. And since that guy ran off with the Staff, I can't get home any other way anyway."

Mom opens her mouth to protest, and I brace myself to have to go back and forth for a while, like when we go out to lunch with my aunts and uncles, and all my relatives insist on paying for the bill. Things got really out of hand once Āh Mā discovered Venmo. But while Mom can be prideful, she's also practical, just like her bàba, and eventually she gives in.

This wasn't the outcome I wanted. Not even close. But if there was never any way that she would return with me after all, I guess it's a lot more than nothing.

TWENTY-TWO

THE BOBA SHOP AT THE END OF THE NETHERWORLD

Since Yama mentioned two kids as the intruders, no one pays attention to Mom and me as we leave her room and I lead her to the elevator. We ride down to the Fifth Court and then head straight for the executive building, where a blue boiler-suited demon custodian is roping off the area where I smashed through the floor with the Staff of Mùlián. Otherwise, the building looks empty, but then we pass Yama's yin-and-yang underworld underlings, Mr. Hēi and Mr. Bái, holding hands as they exit a room with a name plate that reads INFIRMARY. Mr. Bái's eerie white face is streaked with iron, and tiny Mr. Hēi has to stretch up to dab it with a wet tissue.

"Hey, I found—" I start to say, before remembering that I probably shouldn't taunt the people who are in charge in the afterlife now that Mom has to stay here. "I mean, oh no, she found me."

Mr. Hēi glares at me, like he wasn't perfectly happy taking my bribe earlier. "Down the hall," he says. But instead of pointing to Yama's office, he indicates another room that turns out to be a waiting room. To my surprise, I see Kevin sitting in the back and looking bored out of his mind.

"Hey, Evie!" he calls out, waving.

"What? You're still in Dìyù?" It's been hours since we went our separate ways in the Eighth Court—it took at least two just to learn how to weave the thread of fate. If our break-in was such a big deal, why wasn't he escorted to Yama right away instead of being told to sit in the waiting room? Dr. Hsu wasn't kidding about the bureaucracy being really slow down here.

Kevin nods. "Yeah, I've been sitting here for a while. But what are you still—" His eyes light up when he spots my mom behind me. "Hey, you found her!"

An awkward silence follows. Kevin looks back and forth between me and my mom, his brow furrowed in confusion. When Mom sits down next to me, his eyes dart down from her face to the white sweatsuit of all the other dead people in Dìyù. His smile fades, and I know that he's realized what I can't bring myself to say.

The truth is, I wouldn't mind waiting several more hours, so I can just sit with my mom a little longer. But the receptionist demon behind the desk buzzes us in soon after we sit down next to Kevin. When the three of us enter Yama's office, the director is sitting at his desk, still in his pajamas and rasping at his phone.

"What do you mean, someone thrashed Ox-Head and Horse-Face and escaped?" Wait, those are their actual names? "What the Heaven else can go wrong today . . ." Yama's voice trails off as he sees us in his office. I try to keep a straight face as Mom explains to him that she "caught" me. Yama gave his word that anyone who turned us in would go free, but I've seen what justice looks like down here, and I don't want to give our relationship away out of fear he'll take it back just to avoid giving me the satisfaction.

"Very well." Yama turns to the receptionist. "Have her paperwork dealt with *immediately*. She'll have to finish her time in the Court of the Wrongful Dead, but once her risk of becoming a vengeful ghost has been contained, she can go straight to the Tenth Court without further trial."

I can feel the weight of the Spindle in the pocket

of my shorts, which are still underneath my sweatpants. I think Mom's risk of becoming a vengeful ghost is pretty minimal. I'm not sure I'll ever be able to fully accept her decision, but I have to respect it, that she would choose to save her own murderer out of love for her family.

Yama looks at me and Kevin. "Well, since the Staff of Mùlián has exchanged hands"—the director rubs his red temple and lets out an awful-sounding moan of frustration—"Hēi and Bái can escort them to the Tenth Court. You can take Ms. Huang back to her room."

"It's Ms. *Liu* Huang," Mom can't help correcting, like she always does whenever someone leaves out her family name. Yama raises an eyebrow before his eyes light up in recognition. My blood runs cold, remembering his sneer when he threatened to have Kevin's dad thrown into all the Courts.

"Very well. Ms. Liu Huang." The receptionist gestures at Mom to follow her, and my stomach churns. Yama promised that whoever turned us in would go free, but if he realizes she's my own mom, would he take it back out of spite? Because "this is Dìyù"?

But then the director turns to me. "Well, aren't you going to say goodbye to your mother?"

Yama's lip curves upward into a faint smile. "It's not a trap, child," he whispers gently. "Go on."

For a moment, I freeze up, still worried that Yama might go back on his word once I confirm that the woman turning me in isn't a random penitent but the reason I broke in. But then Mom rushes forward and throws her arms around me, and I can't keep myself from hugging her back.

"I love you, Mom," I say, when I finally release her. As awful as this day was, as cruel as it was to be tricked into thinking she was alive and I could bring her home when I can't, I'm glad I got to say it.

Mom pats my pocket, where the Spindle is. "Don't worry, Evie. I know you can do it." I wait for her to add *if you work hard*, but she doesn't. Instead she says, and she's starting to cry now, too, "I love you so much."

I'd thought I was all out of tears, but my eyes have started to sting again. There's so much I want to tell her, but for some reason what comes out is, "Is everything going to be okay?"

Mom doesn't answer for what feels like a long time. I almost tell her to forget it, because of course she has no way of knowing. But then finally she says, her voice gentle but firm, "You will be."

"I promise I'll take care of Mona Li. And Auntie Kathie's baby, too."

"I know you will. Take care of yourself, too."

I watch as the receptionist leads her away. My fingers are still squeezing my red string pendant when a sullen-looking Hēi and Bái arrive to lead Kevin and me to an elevator.

"The boss is too soft," Hēi grumbles, shaking his head as he pushes the very last *4*.

"Soft?" Kevin says in disbelief. "The king, uh, director of Dìyù? The guy who threatened to throw my dad into all the Courts? That guy?"

"Haven't you kids heard of bluffing before? Yama can barely stand to torture the people who deserve it."

Hēi snorts. "You know that mug of molten iron you threw right in Mr. Bái's mug?" His black eyes flash, and Kevin cringes at the memory. "The boss wouldn't stop coming up with excuses to reduce penitents' sentences. Not to take bribes, mind you," he says, shaking his head like that would be a *good* reason, "but because he felt *bad* for the suckers. The bureaucrats up in Heaven didn't care for that, so now he has a punishment of his own down here to remind him to do his job: He has to have liquid metal poured down his throat three times a day."

I remember when I first heard Yama's ravaged voice, how I thought it sounded like his vocal cords had holes poked in them . . . or burned away. My stomach churns.

"So, Yama is being punished for being *too nice*? By *Heaven*?" Kevin blurts out, horrified. As messed up as the supernatural realm is, though, I can't help but feel relief to know that Yama will keep his promise.

The elevator pings—we've arrived in the Tenth Court. Mr. Hēi and Mr. Bái lead us to a stone bridge overlooking a yellow-tinted river, lined with spidery red flowers. A sign hangs over a gate at the bridge's entrance, which Kevin translates: *"Bridge of Helplessness. You are now exiting Dìyù. See you next time!"*

Penitents are lined up in front of the bridge, waiting to cross. But our demonic escorts skip the line and take us straight to the front, to much grumbling from the dead people. In front of the bridge is . . . a boba stall, just like any of the boba shops back in Avalon, right down to a neon sign on a wall reading GRANNY MÈNG PÓ'S FIVE-FLAVOR TEA OF FORGETFULNESS in #aesthetic cursive. So people can share pictures of themselves in the netherworld, I guess.

Behind the counter is an old woman. Instead of a boiler suit, she's dressed in the colorful and chaotic style common to a lot of elderly Asian people I know, as if she just threw on literally whatever was in her closet or could find on sale: in this case, a purple sequined cardigan over a sweater with a cartoon elephant on it and clashing pajama pants, as well as a baseball cap, embroidered with what appears to be a cartoon illustration of herself, over her long sheet of white hair.

"Five-Flavor Tea?" she calls out as she sees us. She reaches toward a stack of plastic cups by the wall, but Mr. Bái puts his hand out as if to say *STOP*. The old woman—I assume she must be Granny Mèng Pó—stares at him blankly, but the only thing that comes out of his mouth is his unnaturally long tongue, which flops out of the side of his face like a fish out of water.

"Oh, we're not dead. We're intruders," Kevin says helpfully. Granny Mèng Pó gives an "Ah!" of understanding.

"You can go straight across the bridge. You better get going fast, before Granny forgets and tries to force-feed you. Sometimes she sips some of her own tea and it makes her a bit senile," Mr. Hēi says, as if we would need to be told to hurry up and get out of Dìyù already. "Good riddance."

He turns to lead Mr. Bái away with a huff, but Kevin shouts after them, "Wait!"

Kevin unzips the handbag and hands the rest of the joss paper dollars we have to Mr. Bái, saying, "I'm really sorry I melted your face."

I stare at him in disbelief. Maybe Yama isn't such a bad guy, but everyone else here seems perfectly happy or totally unconcerned about torturing people for a living. But then I decide to keep my opinion to myself. If it makes Kevin feel better, you know what, that's fine.

As soon as Hēi and Bái have left, we make it onto the Bridge of Helplessness. The bridge is a simple stone arch, extending out over dark water with an unsettling yellow tint. A dense, sickly yellow fog hangs in the air, obscuring the end of the bridge. A faint breeze ripples through the blood-red, spider-like flowers on the banks of the river.

"So why is there a tea shop at the end of Dìyù?" I ask, just to break the silence. I still feel numb about having to say goodbye to Mom again after I'd found her.

Behind us, more penitents are lined up in front of Granny Mèng Pó's boba stall. Despite presumably being a supernatural being like the other Dìyù personnel, she walks like a regular slow old person. The crowd is obviously getting impatient. When Granny Mèng Pó makes it halfway across the floor of the little shop, she suddenly stops and slaps her forehead. "Āiyā! Silly Granny! I forgot the tea." Chuckling, she turns back around and begins walking very slowly back to the counter. Penitents erupt into a chorus of groans; someone cries out, "We're going to be stuck here forever!"

"Oh! I know the answer to this!" says Kevin. "The tea is to wipe away any memories of people's past lives before they leave Dìyù and are reincarnated into their next life. I watched this drama where the couple didn't drink the tea and that's why they were still soulmates in the next life."

All of a sudden, I get a queasy feeling in the pit of my stomach. I'd known that Mom was going to get another life after her time is up in Dìyù, but I hadn't really thought about the fact that she wouldn't get to take the memories from *this* one with her. Meaning she would have no memory of her family. Of me.

I guess it's a good thing she doesn't have to remember this place. And she'd be a different person anyway, living a different life. But it still makes me sad. After her time in the Fourth Court is over, she'll really be gone.

"Hey, I'm sorry," Kevin says after a while, startling me out of my thoughts. "I was really hoping you would bring her back."

I take a deep breath, which I regret instantly as I suck in a big mouthful of foul river fumes. Though the menacingly beautiful blood-red spider-flowers turn out to have a gentle fragrance that evens it out a little. "Me too," I say. "I'm sorry you spent all day in Dìyù for nothing."

Kevin shrugs. "I wouldn't say it's for nothing."

Right. I couldn't bring my mom home, but he got to know he does indeed have a soulmate, just like his parents did. So it all worked out pretty well for one of us.

I can taste my bitterness in my mouth, even though I want to be genuinely happy for him. But then it hits me that it wasn't all for nothing for me, either, not really. Because as hard as it was to say goodbye to my mom for the last time, if that was the price of getting to spend a little more time with her, I'd do it all over again.

"You're right," I admit. "It wasn't."

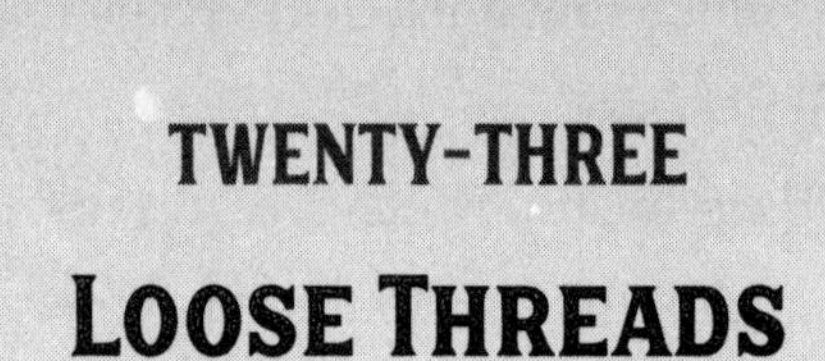

TWENTY-THREE
LOOSE THREADS

Exiting Dìyù is the weirdest thing. One moment we're walking on the stone bridge, the fog too dense to see the end of it or what's on the opposite shore. And then the next thing I know, the yellow fog is gone and I'm back in my Auntie Kathie's living room.

The lights are all on, so it must be evening now. The living room is empty, but I can hear the Council of Elders still talking in the next room. They must have decided to stay with Auntie Kathie after my mom's body was found. My poor aunt must be worried out of her mind about me.

But for a moment, my feet can't bring themselves to go in there. I just stay put until, to my surprise, Thida comes out from the bathroom.

"Eevee!" She runs forward and throws her arms

around me. Not a forced hug where she doesn't seem to know what to do with her arms, a real hug.

"Dude, I'm so glad to see you. I was so . . ." Thida's voice trails off, and she says simply, "I'm so sorry."

She doesn't say anything else, and she doesn't have to. There's so much I'll have to tell my best friend later, but right now I just want to be sad.

Thida lowers her voice. "Evie, I'm really sorry you have to deal with this nonsense now, but, uh, just a heads-up . . . after your aunt got—after your aunt got the news, she was really upset and got a lot of phone calls from people, and—"

But whatever she was about to tell me is drowned out by an ear-piercing scream. "EVIE!" Auntie Kathie sprints into the living room, or at least, the fastest a woman in the advanced stages of pregnancy can sprint.

"Evie! I was so, so worried about you. I swear I could kill you." Auntie Kathie squeezes me so hard I almost think she will.

When she finally lets go of me, she notices Kevin. "I didn't forget," she says, even though Kevin didn't ask. "Marcus Morby."

Kevin furrows his brow, puzzled. "Who?"

"That's who your red thread of fate is tied to. He's

two years younger than you and lives in Texas. The rest, I'll leave for you to find out. I hope he deserves you, kiddo. I really do."

All the life is gone from my aunt's voice, like she's been hollowed out. But Kevin's eyes burst wide open as he realizes what she just told him.

"Oh, shoot!" he says, then furrows his brow again. "Wait, so I'm bi? That's awesome!"

"Dude, read the room," Thida says. But I'm only half listening to their conversation, because I'm staring at the man who just walked into the room and beside Auntie Kathie. He's not one of the Elders—he's only around thirty-five. He's handsome—not like K-pop idol handsome, but in kind of a rough way—but that's not why I'm staring. It's his eyes. At first I think he's wearing eyeliner, but when he comes closer, I realize he just has naturally long eyelashes. Suddenly I remember a stray remark my mom made over pancakes at the 24-hour diner: She said that a set of pretty eyelashes was going to be the downfall of my aunt.

"Oh. This is my—" Auntie Kathie pauses, looking a little embarrassed. But I don't miss how her right hand sweeps over her belly in the moment's hesitation over what to call the guy. It could be a coincidence, but then he moves closer and puts his hand on her belly, too, and my stomach sinks all the way to Dìyù as my suspicion is confirmed.

"Well, we're figuring it out," she says finally, and my blood turns cold. "But he came over after . . ."

Auntie Kathie bursts into tears, and The Gambler wraps his arms around her waist. I want to yell at him to get his murderous hands off my aunt. No, I want to go back to Dìyù *again* just so I can drag him back there myself.

"Hey, what happened to you two?" With a jolt, I realize The Gambler is talking to me. Kevin and I are still coated with blood from the neck up, and though it's dry, we must look—well, like we just got back from Hell.

"Oh, they're fine," Auntie Kathie says quickly, wiping her face and trying her best to compose herself. "This is my niece, Evie. She just got back from, ah, community theater."

The Gambler's piercing eyes flash at the word *niece*, as he realizes he's looking at the daughter of the woman he murdered. "Showbiz, huh?" he says. "You must take after your auntie."

He holds out his hand, and my promise to my mom feels like a chain around me. Am I really supposed to just stand here, watching the man who *killed my mom* with his hands on my sobbing and vulnerable aunt, and not say anything?

But then I look at my Auntie Kathie, and I remember that as horrible as it is that I have to save this man, the alternative would destroy my aunt's life—and that of my cousin. As painful as it is, until I've finished his new thread of fate, I can't tell her the truth.

But, I realize slowly, that doesn't mean I have to just shut my mouth and let my mom's death go unpunished. I don't need the Spindle to ensure her murderer sees justice. It'll be difficult when I can't let my aunt find out—which means I won't be able to tell the authorities or the Guilds, either. But that just means I'll have to find a way on my own. I just inherited one of the most powerful magic items in the world . . . *and* my mom's list of people who owe our family a favor.

So, even though it hurts inside, I smile back and shake the hand of the man who killed my mother.

I did promise her that I wouldn't pursue revenge. But it wouldn't be the first time I didn't listen to my mom.

ACKNOWLEDGMENTS

First, I have to thank Dhonielle Clayton for giving me this incredible opportunity, and for all the work you do to bring diverse voices to children's books—especially at this moment, when so many adults are trying to ban them. As disheartening as that has been, your fearlessness and leadership in this fight give me hope, and I am grateful and honored that you trusted me with Evie's story.

Thanks to my family: My dad, for raising me to love books and stories, and for encouraging me to pursue my dream. My mom, for your unconditional love and strength. My brother, Stanley, my first and best friend: For all the stories we've bonded over (both ours and others'), for always being willing to discuss my plot ideas and jokes, and for your unwavering support and faith in me. And of course to Umma, who gives so much love and takes no nonsense, and who I still want to be when I grow up.

Thanks to the entire team at Cake Creative Kitchen, including John Morgan and Kate Sullivan for your invaluable feedback on *Spindle*'s sample pages. Thank you to Clay Morrell, Shelly Romero, Carlyn

Greenwald, and Haneen Oriqat for all your hard work in bringing Evie's story to life, and to Suzie Townsend for helping this book find a home. Thank you to Anna Roberto and the team at Macmillan: Jean Feiwel, Starr Baer, Kim Waymer, Aurora Parlagreco, and Morgan Rath. Thank you to Kiuyan Ran for the absolutely stunning cover art. And thank you to Erin Siu and Lynn Lawrence-Brown, who provided notes on the Chinese language and cultural authenticity. Any mistakes that remain are my own.

To my friends and writer friends: Amanda Huynh, Nhi Ha, Dani Lee, Daka Hermon, and Goldie Shen. Goldie, you and your family also get a shout-out for checking my Chinese translations so I didn't embarrass myself to the authenticity readers.

Finally, I want to thank Hayley Chewins, Gail D. Villanueva, K.C. Held, Judy I. Lin, and R.C. Lewis, who very generously offered their time and mentorship at various points in my journey to publication.

Thank you for reading this Feiwel & Friends book.
The friends who made

THE SPINDLE OF FATE

possible are:

Jean Feiwel, Publisher
Liz Szabla, VP, Associate Publisher
Rich Deas, Senior Creative Director
Anna Roberto, Executive Editor
Holly West, Senior Editor
Kat Brzozowski, Senior Editor
Dawn Ryan, Executive Managing Editor
Kim Waymer, Senior Production Manager
Foyinsi Adegbonmire, Editor
Rachel Diebel, Editor
Emily Settle, Editor
Brittany Groves, Assistant Editor
Aurora Parlagreco, Associate Art Director
Starr Baer, Production Editor